HARPER NOVEL OF SUSPENSE

THE COME-ON

A JOAN KAHN BOOK

THE
COME-ON

~~~⌇~~~

Margaret Yorke

Harper & Row, Publishers
New York, Hagerstown, San Francisco, London

All the characters and events in this story are imaginary.

This work was first published in England under the title *The Point of Murder*.

A HARPER NOVEL OF SUSPENSE

FIRST U.S. EDITION

Copy editor: Mildred Maynard

Library of Congress Cataloging in Publication Data

Yorke, Margaret.
   The come-on.

   I.   Title.
PZ4.Y643Cm   1979   [PR6075.07] 823'.9'14
ISBN 0-06-014774-1   78-69513

79 80 81 82 83 10 9 8 7 6 5 4 3 2 1

1

In the front bedroom of No. 11 Chestnut Avenue, Ferringham, Mrs. Maud Wilson was waiting. A commercial was showing on the television screen before her. When the main program began, so would the radio concert which her daughter Kate planned to hear. At that instant, Mrs. Wilson would ring her bell to demand white bread and butter instead of the wholemeal on her supper tray—punishment for the brisk way in which the tray had been set down because Kate did not want to miss a note of the overture.

Though old, Mrs. Wilson was not ill. She had chosen never to recover from the shock of Kate's conception and birth when Mrs. Wilson herself was forty-four years old and had long since abandoned hope of a replacement for the son who had died in infancy fifteen years before, and whose round face and mild unfocused gaze stared at Kate from photographs dotted round the house: the tyrant presence mentioned daily by her mother in the context of "if only."

If only he were alive, Kate thought grimly as she answered her mother's summons. He would have combined, their mother declared, a perfect disposition with good looks and an acute business sense; penny-pinching would long ago have been exchanged for a return to luxury. Kate remembered the treats and comforts which money had provided in her father's lifetime: holidays in expensive hotels, visits to London with theatres and dinner afterward. He had died suddenly while Kate was still at school, leaving a drapery business that had been unprofitable for years. When the financial truth was discovered, Kate had felt betrayed as well as bereaved, but now, after over twenty years alone with her mother, she understood why he had not shared his problems.

The overture to *The Magic Flute* went unheard on Kate's radio in her small sitting room, once the breakfast room, as she angrily buttered two slices of white bread.

She had just sat down after taking them upstairs when the bell rang again.

"My eyes are tired tonight. Will you turn the color up, Kate?" Mrs. Wilson requested in suffering tones.

Kate moved the control on the television.

"Too bright," said Mrs. Wilson.

When at last Kate was allowed to go, the color was exactly as it had been before she made any adjustment.

But tomorrow was Friday, and a special Friday.

Twice weekly, on Wednesdays and Fridays, Mrs. Burke came to clean and stayed all day. On those days Kate did not have to rush home from work to get her mother's lunch, and at intervals of two or three months Mrs. Burke stayed for the weekend, and Kate went away.

2

She spent these weekends with her friend Betty Davenport in the country. At least, her mother thought she did.

In the morning, Mrs. Wilson complained of a headache, then a pain in her side. She always developed ailments when Kate was going away and conducted her war of nerves until Mrs. Burke, who came early on Fridays, arrived to soothe her. Fortunately for Mrs. Burke, Mrs. Wilson enjoyed a change of company; few people visited her these days, and since Mrs. Burke was not subjected to the torments Mrs. Wilson devised for her daughter, she found her charge easy to manage and enjoyed watching color television with her.

"Kate's just at the end of the telephone, if you're not well and want her to come home," said Mrs. Burke.

"I'm sure I don't want to interfere with your pleasures, Kate," Mrs. Wilson said, sighing, as Kate left quickly.

Once, Kate would have let her mother's act upset her. When she was younger, she had worried while away lest her mother fall critically ill in her absence. By now, she accepted that the old lady might live ten or more complaining years, with nothing altered except that Kate would be that much older, too. She often dreamed about what she would do when release finally came. The house would fetch a good price, although it had never been modernized. Ferringham, once a small country town, had developed several light industries and it lay between two motorways, where property and building land were always in demand. As a child, Kate had wandered over fields and woods behind the house, but now it was surrounded by new housing projects. Ten years ago, a builder had bought part of the Wilsons'

3

garden, and three houses stood on what had once been a tennis court and shrubbery. Mrs. Wilson had paid for the exterior painting of the house with part of the proceeds; she had bought an annuity with the rest. Any interior decorating was done by Kate.

In the early years, Kate had tried to persuade her mother to sell the house, but Mrs. Wilson would demand pathetically, "Am I to lose my home as well as everything else?" She ignored Kate's insistence that a flat would cost less to run and could be kept warm. Later, in spite of the cold, the inconvenience, and the cost, Kate was glad of the space which allowed each of them her territories. Kate's areas were the kitchen, the erstwhile breakfast room, and her own bedroom; the rest of the house was her mother's, but now Mrs. Wilson seldom used the large, drafty drawing room, heated only by a gas fire, because she rarely came downstairs.

One day, Kate knew, she would travel. In her bedroom, a big room with a high, old-fashioned single bed, a large mahogany wardrobe and dressing table, and a worn blue Axminster carpet surrounded by varnished floorboards, there was a whole drawer full of brochures advertising trips to Persia, India, and Japan. Kate constantly collected new ones, writing in reply to newspaper advertisements; she spent hours planning trips she might never make, until—

But sometimes she did escape.

It had begun seven years ago. Until then, Kate really had spent occasional weekends with Betty Davenport. She had gradually lost touch with her other school friends, all now married or far away, but while Betty's husband, Jack, was in the R.A.F., Kate and Betty had kept in touch, and when he had retired and bought a small holding in Gloucestershire, it was natural for Betty to invite Kate over. She was a popular guest, helping wherever aid was most needed: with the outside work in the developing market garden; in the kitchen; or with the children. She was good with children, for she met plenty in her job.

At first she had been able to leave her mother alone for a night, with a cold meal prepared for the evening and Mrs. Burke coming in by day, but her mother displayed martyrdom over carrying her tray from the larder into the dining room, which she insisted on using; rising from the sofa, where she spent most of her time, required such effort.

Kate never remembered her mother being active; she and her father, off on jaunts together, had felt like children playing truant from school as they left the quiet house. In the last year of his life, she had gone with him to several dinner parties he had given in Ferringham's Royal Hotel, since her mother could not or would not entertain his business friends. The guests had all been nice to Kate and had flattered her. Then he had died, leaving no insurance and the business in debt.

Kate never liked to remember that.

"Thank goodness *my* father provided for me," her mother often said.

Mrs. Wilson had a small private income of her own, but her husband had been generous in life, so that she had spent little of it and had invested the rest. Now, with inflation, it did not go far, but the capital was still untouched. Sometimes Mrs. Wilson spoke of selling out to increase her annuity; if she were to do that, only the house would be left for Kate.

Kate was secretary, receptionist, and general prop to a group practice of doctors in the town. She had been with them for fifteen years, first when the surgery was in an old house in the High Street, now at the new Health Centre. When her father died, Kate was at Ferringham Grammar School and hoped to go

5

on to university, but had not opposed her mother's decree that this plan must be abandoned. She could be a passenger no longer, Mrs. Wilson said. An uncle, since dead, had provided funds for a crash course at a secretarial college and had helped the lawyers sort out what could be rescued from the sale of the shop after the debts were paid; then, his duty done, he had left his wearisome sister-in-law and his pale, dull niece to make the best of things, and had returned to Southampton, where he ran a pub.

As soon as Kate's secretarial training ended, Mrs. Burke's daily visits were cut to two a week. The resident cook had been dismissed at once. Kate began work in a solicitor's office, and stayed there four years. Quite soon, she thought of becoming articled and qualifying as a solicitor herself, but she still had much to learn about her mother and, unwisely, she mentioned the idea. Almost immediately, Mrs. Wilson complained of feeling acutely ill.

Dr. Wetherbee, called in, was unable to diagnose the precise trouble, though he had no illusions about Mrs. Wilson's chronic invalidism; certainly the patient now had palpitations and no appetite, so Kate had to take time off from the office and forgo her holiday. After her mother's slow recovery, she felt it was useless to entertain ambitions of her own, though Dr. Wetherbee urged her to persevere.

"I wouldn't stick at it," Kate said. "I wouldn't be able to."

If her mother knew she was studying at home in the evenings, she would be ridiculed and interrupted. Lawrence, her brother, had been the one with the brains, Mrs. Wilson would say, as she so often did, though how one could assess the intelligence of a three-month-old baby was a mystery to Kate.

To his partner, Richard Stearne, Dr. Wetherbee deplored Kate's attitude.

"But she can't help it, poor girl. It's her mother—a war of

attrition. She's always on at Kate, nagging her about her appearance—about being too tall—and her clumsiness, though I've never noticed that, I must say," he added.

Dr. Stearne had visited Mrs. Wilson several times in Dr. Wetherbee's absence; he scarcely knew Kate.

"Perhaps she'll get married," he said.

"To whom? No one will run the gantlet of the mother," said Dr. Wetherbee.

Over the years, he was proved right. Kate had few opportunities to meet young people socially, though for some years she did play tennis at the local club and was fetched by her mixed-doubles partner from the house in Chestnut Avenue. She played rather well; her height made her hard to pass at the net and she had a powerful service. People were keen to partner her on the court, but no one wanted to marry her.

When their secretary-*cum*-receptionist retired, the two doctors offered Kate her job.

Richard Stearne was against the idea at first. By now, he had visited No. 11 often enough to understand the situation.

"It'll sap what little initiative she has," he argued.

"She may be happier," said Dr. Wetherbee.

He almost added that Kate was doomed, in any case. Mrs. Wilson, as far as he could judge, though muscularly fragile, was likely to live a long time. Her heart was strong, since it had seldom been exposed to strain.

Kate joined the doctors, and when, a year later, Paul Fox arrived as third partner, she fell in love with him.

On Friday morning, Kate drove her old green Mini to the Health Centre and parked in her usual spot. She was, as always, ahead of the doctors, but the cleaner was there, just finishing off.

Kate removed her head scarf, hung up her shabby beige raincoat, shook out her beige-colored hair, and put on her white uniform. It was too soon to let anticipation fill her; it did not do to look forward to things too much, lest the hand of fate intervene to prevent the expected pleasure.

Seven years ago, Dr. Wetherbee had, one Friday, been unable to drive himself to a medical conference in Birmingham, where he went regularly, because he had broken his ankle skiing; it was his first injury in twenty winter sports holidays, and not his fault, since someone had collided with him. It was making his work difficult; the other doctors were having to make most of his calls.

"You take me, Kate," he said. His wife, a kind, plump woman and now a busy grandmother, did not drive.

"Me? But I couldn't," said Kate.

"Why not?"

"Mother," said Kate automatically. It was her instant response to any new idea.

"We'll only be gone for the day," Dr. Wetherbee said. "And it's Friday—your mother will have Mrs. Burke with her anyway." Dr. Wetherbee knew the details of Kate's domestic arrangements. "You should get out more," he added. He'd been meaning to say so for some time. Kate's annual holiday consisted of taking her mother to Paignton for two weeks in July.

"You wouldn't be comfortable in my car," Kate said. Dr. Wetherbee was tall and bulky, and there was the plastered foot.

"We'll take the Rover," said Dr. Wetherbee.

"But I couldn't drive it," said Kate.

"You could. It's perfectly simple," he said. "Don't be silly, Kate. You'll enjoy it. You can have a look round the shops while I'm at the meeting. Marjorie Dodds will put in a few more hours, I'm sure, so don't say you can't be spared."

Two married women, Marjorie Dodds and Nora Ford, worked part-time at the Health Centre helping with the telephone, clinics, and evening surgeries; much of Kate's work was behind the scenes coping with forms and records and typing letters dictated onto tape in the doctors' spare moments.

Kate was overruled. It was Dr. Wetherbee who had insisted that she learn to drive, and he had helped Kate to buy her first car, a fourth-hand one, advancing a loan on her salary; in those days such cars could be bought cheaply. Until then, Kate had bicycled to work and back, as there was no direct bus from Chestnut Avenue across the town to the Health Centre. The car made a great difference to her journeys, especially in the middle of the day, hurrying back to get her mother's lunch; but Mrs. Wilson thought it a shocking extravagance until she realized that now Kate could take her out for drives. She complained then about the quality of Kate's vehicle but offered no financial aid to buy a better one.

Once she got used to the size of the car, Kate enjoyed driving Dr. Wetherbee's Rover. On the way back from Birmingham after his meeting, he said they would stop for dinner. He had given Kate two pounds for her lunch, a lot in those days, and she had attempted to hand him back the change. She had eaten in a department store after buying some stockings for her mother and a length of material to make herself a skirt; she was too tall to buy ready-made clothes easily.

"Keep it, Kate, and get your hair done or buy some frippery," said Dr. Wetherbee absently. "We'll stop at the Bridge Hotel. I usually do."

The Bridge Hotel was small and the atmosphere was friendly. Dr. Wetherbee ordered their meal with the calm confidence of experience and the knowledge that he could afford to pay. Kate was reminded of the times she had dined like this with her father. The waiter had pulled out her chair for her as she sat down; when they left, he released her again. She was helped into her coat, a

9

beige raincoat, predecessor to the one she wore now and still kept in the back of the car for emergencies.

Little courtesies, she thought; how very nice. People doing things for one's comfort. Manners. She played the evening through in her mind in bed that night, and after a straight run with Dr. Wetherbee in his own role, she replaced him with Paul Fox. In that dream, she fell asleep.

The idea developed from that day.

First, Kate took Dr. Wetherbee's advice about having her hair done; hitherto, she had lopped it herself and tied it at the nape of her neck, out of the way—like a schoolgirl, she now realized. She went to Jeanne's in the High Street for restyling, and emerged bouffant.

Her mother was caustic.

"You look ridiculous," she said.

But Kate knew her appearance was improved, and she had enjoyed sitting in the warm salon, ministered to by Jeanne with her scissors and rollers, and soft towels. Now she went regularly, though the results never lasted long, and on Fridays when she was going away she had a lunchtime appointment at Jeanne's.

At first she thought only of spending a night where it would be warm and comfortable: where she could lie in the bath for an hour, if she liked, without the water running cold; and where people would look after her. To her collection of holiday brochures, Kate began to add those which advertised weekend breaks. Everything came by post, and there was no risk of discovery because the mail always arrived before she left for work. She wrote, guilty about the money spent on stamps, for brochures about other things, too: modern kitchens; mail-order offers; labor-saving gadgets; even encyclopedias and cookery books.

Through a brochure Kate discovered The Black Swan at Risely.

It was by the river not far from the Bridge Hotel, where she and Dr. Wetherbee had dined, and seemed reassuringly similar. Now she had to find the money, and the courage to go away on her own. She saved slowly to achieve the first, skimping on the housekeeping wherever she could and cutting down on her lunches on the days when she did not go home, and she gave up her Sunday glass of sherry. For the second, she had to become someone else; not gawky, tall Kate Wilson, but a woman of poise.

A patient who disposed of her own misfits and bad buys at a quality secondhand dress shop in Ferringham called Bargain Boutique had told Kate that she would find the shop sold model clothes in her size. She went there and acquired a nucleus wardrobe, first a suit and then an evening dress, and she bought new make-up following the advice of a magazine she read at Jeanne's.

Mrs. Havant, a widow, was born.

2

Gary Browne (he had added the "e" himself) combed his hair carefully in front of the mirror in the gents'. It was thick and curly, of a mid-brown shade, and many girls had eagerly run their hands through it. He set his tie straight, shrugged his shoulders comfortably into his jacket, and prepared to leave. He had finished his business calls for the day and was off in search of talent; with luck he need not return tonight to his own narrow bed in the Grange Residential Hotel in Wattleton. Gary sold encyclopedias and much of his wages depended on commission, but he had a persuasive manner and often got "yes" in the end where first a firm "no" had been said, and not only in the matter of sales, he reflected complacently, though there had been one or two rather unfortunate incidents in that connection better not remembered: chicks changing their minds.

He had moved about a lot after he stopped working for his father, a jobbing builder in Nottingham. He had sold shirts, been a cinema projectionist, run a record shop, and had a short spell in an accountant's office, which ended when he was caught borrowing from the petty cash. Gary had not yet found his niche, and his present job was just a way of marking time on the way to the brilliant future he envisaged. Meanwhile, he spent money on the pools and on backing horses. One day, he knew he would win enough to plunge into property: first a house, which he'd do up and turn into bed-sits, tasteful but cheap—he'd got all the know-how—and then he'd move on to the big stuff until he owned an apartment block with a penthouse suite for himself and a dolly to match.

He went back to his car, which was parked in a lay-by near the public convenience, a secluded one in the shelter of some trees on the edge of a park. There had been another car there when he arrived, an old green Mini, but it was gone now. Kate had finished transforming herself into Mrs. Havant in the ladies' section of the same public convenience a few minutes before.

She had chosen the name Havant because her father was born in Havant, in Hampshire. Her grandfather had been a petty officer in the Royal Navy.

With her hair still slightly rigid under a film of lacquer, Kate drove northward, already out of her role as a dutiful daughter and now a chic widow going eagerly to meet her married lover. At last it was safe to admit the feeling of eagerness; she had not been away since November. After some miles, she saw a small blue Fiat ahead of her, limping along. Judging by the angle of the car, she decided it had a flat tire, and as she caught up she could see that a rear wheel was down; the driver—a woman, though you could not always be certain from behind—must surely be aware that something was wrong. In fact, on the next straight stretch, she pulled in to the roadside.

Kate's first instinct as she passed was to drive on, for she did not want to be late, but her work involved helping people and it was against her nature to ignore someone else's predicament. She stopped, too, backed up to the Fiat, and got out.

A pretty young woman with short dark hair, and long slender legs well displayed under her tight skirt, was already fitting a wheel brace to a nut on the hub of the car. The jack lay ready to be placed in position. Perhaps no aid would be needed. Years ago, Kate had taken evening classes in car maintenance, though she had never finished the course; she did, however, know how to change the wheel of a car, and so did this girl.

"Can you manage?" Kate asked.

"Yes, thanks," said the girl.

Kate watched. The girl was slight, and undoing the nuts sometimes needed muscle. Sure enough, the first the girl tried would not budge. Nor would the second.

"Let me have a go," said Kate, conscious of her good suit, her clean hands, and her now varnished nails.

She loosened two nuts but the others remained fixed.

"Oh, dear," said Kate, and glanced at her watch.

"You go on. Someone else will stop," said the girl.

Kate wavered.

"I could send help," she said. "I'm only going to The Black Swan at Risely. That's the next village. There's a garage there."

"No, I'm sure that's not necessary," said the girl. "Someone else will stop." It would be rude to point out that she stood more chance alone of being rescued by a passing knight of the road.

As she thought this, another car drew up behind them. A male head was thrust through the window and a cheerful voice spoke.

"Well, ladies, want any help?" asked Gary Browne, smiling at the girl.

Kate saw bright brown eyes, rather close together, under thick, wavy matching hair, neatly arranged, as the young man stepped from his Ford Escort. He wore a well-pressed suit, and

14

she noticed a lavender tie; he looked completely respectable. She had not a qualm as she drove off, leaving Sandra King with the man who killed her later that night.

Kate's hands had got oily helping the girl, but she kept some tissue wipes in the car, so that she was able to clean the worst of it off before she entered the hotel as the usual poised Mrs. Havant they were accustomed to see several times a year.

The old porter came out to take her case.

"Nice to see you again, madam," he said, and Kate followed him upstairs to a room she had had before. It was large, and overlooked the gardens sloping down to the river.

She enjoyed having time to savor everything, particularly the leisurely bath in water scented with expensive bath oil, a gift from a patient that had lasted for several such weekends. She liked wrapping herself in the soft white towel—a clean one provided each day—and walking around in bare feet on the thick carpet. She put on a long black dress, which its original owner, a Ferringham business magnate's wife, had given to her daily help, who had sold it at once to Bargain Boutique. With the lacquer brushed out of her hair, her eyelids lightly shadowed, rouge on her pale skin, and wearing a soft pink lipstick, she was a totally different creature from the dowdy woman who had left Chestnut Avenue that morning.

It was the change in her personality that had intrigued Richard Stearne. He had been astonished when he called at The Black Swan for dinner one Friday evening, on the way back from a medical conference, and saw her. She was sitting at a corner table, the light from a candle giving her an added softness, and his first thought was: What an attractive woman. Next, he felt there was something familiar about her, and that she must be a patient whom he could not at once name, or even a medical colleague.

Kate, who had seen him come in, felt her heart thudding with fright. She bent her head over her plate, scrutinizing the black swan painted on its rim, and put her ringed left hand on the table. He would not recognize her; she must just keep calm. Meanwhile, the waiter led Richard to a distant table and she was out of his direct vision.

She finished her meal quickly and fled from the restaurant.

It was as he ate his cheese and biscuits that Richard realized the woman reminded him of Kate. He asked the waiter if he knew who she was.

"Oh, yes, sir. That's Mrs. Havant. She's one of our regulars— been coming here for several years now. A very nice lady," said the waiter.

Hiding in her room instead of having coffee in the lounge, Kate told herself that Richard wouldn't think anything of one old green Mini in the hotel yard if he noticed it as he left; he probably didn't even know the number of hers. She had made a bad slip, however, when arranging this weekend; it coincided with one of the meetings at which Richard now took Dr. Wetherbee's place.

But Richard did recognize the number of her car.

It was chance that had taken him, that evening, to The Black Swan. Like Dr. Wetherbee, he usually stopped at the Bridge Hotel, but that evening he was late and it was busy; he would have had to wait for a table, so he drove on to the next likely spot; it was as simple as that.

Kate lay sleepless for a long time that night. Often she had played such a scene in her mind, running on to recognition with the words "You look so different, somehow" being uttered in husky tones by Paul Fox.

Paul, the third partner in the group, was a large, confident man. He had gone through medical school carelessly breaking

16

the hearts of vulnerable nurses, and when he came to Ferringham he broke Kate's with the same casual negligence.

"Kate, darling, you're wonderful," he would cry, seizing her round the waist and whirling her about. He was a keen rugby player; the feel of his strong, muscular arms, and the sight of his fresh, healthy face with the shining blue eyes so close, excited Kate. Paul never intended to lead her on; her starved imagination snatched at crumbs so that she believed his insincere compliments, repeating them endlessly to herself and equipping them with profound significance, though Paul forgot them as soon as they were uttered. She stayed on after his surgeries, tidying things pointlessly for the chance of a word alone, risking her mother's ire when she was late home. Paul took it for granted; women had always gone out of their way to render him services, small and large, and he rewarded Kate with more of his smiles and an occasional uncaring peck on the cheek. Sometimes, when he was going there anyway, he took her to the pub on the corner for a beer. To him, Kate was a pleasant, dull girl, a good sort and efficient, like many another he had known. She was a good listener, and he related tales of his rugger triumphs at these off-duty meetings. He never asked her about herself.

Dr. Wetherbee and Richard Stearne were aware of Kate's infatuation. It was impossible to miss how she blushed when Paul appeared; her response to his teasing; her pathetic sartorial forays into fashions which did not suit her, though they were covered most of the time by her white coat.

Kate brought flowers from the garden for Paul's office. They made his hay-fever patients sneeze, and he asked her, pleasantly enough, to stop. She put them in the waiting room after that, but they were really still for him.

Then Paul had married Nancy very suddenly. The first anyone in Ferringham knew about his plans was when he invited the Health Centre staff to his wedding.

Kate's mother provided a cast-iron excuse for Kate's refusing the invitation. By the time Paul came back from his honeymoon in Ibiza, a cold calm had replaced her misery. Paul would regret his marriage one day, or Nancy would desert him. When calamity came, Kate would still be there.

But Nancy did not desert Paul. She produced three sons and she helped with some of the clinics. And eventually Mrs. Havant's life began.

On the Monday after Richard had seen her at The Black Swan, he looked at Kate with new interest. Her hair had resumed its usual limpness; her face had its normal pallor. But she was a dark horse: she must be meeting someone—Mr. Havant presumably—at the hotel. Yet she had been dining alone. What was she up to?

"Had a good weekend, Kate?" Richard asked her. "You went away, didn't you?" He was looking through the letters she had already sorted and put ready for him.

"Yes, very nice," she said, and her heart began to thump again.

"Your friend was well?"

"Yes, thanks." Under her white coat the pounding heart must be visible, Kate felt, but she remained outwardly calm.

"Good." Richard looked at her then and smiled. He had large hazel eyes behind spectacles, and was a little bald. "Good," he repeated, and returned to his mail.

He said no more. Why spoil her fun? She got little enough respite from that old dragon at home. But he was very curious.

The next time Kate went to The Black Swan, she doubly checked Richard's diary to make sure that he had no conference to bring him through Risely while she was there.

One slid into things so easily, Richard reflected, driving to Risely to meet Kate. A middle-aged man's one-night stand with a pretty girl was much easier to explain than his own entanglement.

Neither he nor Kate was in love with the other, but then wasn't romantic love an invention to lend sexual passion respectability? There was, however, deep affection and trust between them now, and he still found her Mrs. Havant personality fascinating.

When he had discovered it, he had meant to leave her to it, thinking good luck to her with whatever she was doing. Then, one Saturday, when she had departed the previous evening ostensibly to her Gloucestershire friend, he found himself unexpectedly alone, off duty, and with a planned game of golf canceled because of bad weather. Cynthia, his wife, had gone on a weekend's cookery and flower-arranging course; she had needed urging, knowing he would be free from calls that weekend, but each encouraged the other to pursue interests they did not share, like Richard's golf and Cynthia's bridge. Philip, their son, was spending the weekend with a school friend.

Richard had a whole afternoon and evening to himself—the next day, too, come to that. He could use the time to catch up on unread medical journals; he could read a novel; he might go to the cinema. For some reason, none of these ideas appealed; instead, a devilish impulse sent him out in his car to Risely.

It was spring, and the first pale green leaves were appearing on the willows that bordered the river as he drove into the yard behind The Black Swan. Kate's car was there. What would she be doing now? It was midafternoon. Richard felt suddenly mean. He would embarrass her if they met. He nearly turned to drive away, but why not go into the hotel for tea? He could pretend not to recognize Kate. He might not see her; she might be in bed with her lover.

The very idea made him want to laugh. Kate, of all people! It must be some married man, but how had she ever found him? And was he responsible for her transformation? For transformed she had been, that other time, into a very desirable woman.

When Richard walked into the lounge of The Black Swan that

wet spring afternoon, Kate was sitting there lost in a novel borrowed from the library, safe from the interruptions which beset her, whatever she tried to enjoy, at home. She sensed rather than saw Richard and, looking up, was lost. Her face went white, and her mouth made a round O, though no sound escaped.

Richard sat down beside her.

"Hullo, Kate," he said. "What are you reading?" and then he quickly added, "It's all right, don't be alarmed. I won't give you away, Mrs. Havant."

"I'll explain," said Kate wildly, her Mrs. Havant façade slipping.

"No need." Richard was ashamed now of spying on her.

"No, I must. You'll understand," Kate said, knowing in that moment that he would.

In the end, since it had stopped raining, they went for a walk. Mrs. Havant possessed no stout shoes, but Kate Wilson kept boots in the back of her car because she sometimes delivered medicines to patients in country areas. Kate Wilson's beige raincoat was in the car, too, and she put that on, but it was Mrs. Havant's smart hairdo that Richard saw before him as they went in single file down a narrow path to the river.

They walked a long way while Kate, never once looking at him, explained, even describing her trips to Bargain Boutique. Richard was amazed and moved. No man was involved at all; this was just a lonely woman seeking comfort.

"They're nice here, the staff. Some of them have been here years. They know me now. It's easy," Kate said. "I don't go into the bar, or anything like that. I have a glass of wine with dinner, though," she added defiantly.

By the time they got back, it was too late for tea. Richard stayed for a drink. Then he stayed to dinner, too. While he washed in the men's room, Kate went upstairs and changed into

Mrs. Havant's long black dinner dress. She led the way to her table in the restaurant and said to the headwaiter, "Two tonight, please."

Richard watched her with amused admiration. He took over, though, at dinner, and ordered a bottle of claret.

"Mrs. Havant is my guest tonight," he told the waiter, and he made Kate choose from the à-la-carte menu instead of the set menu of the bargain weekend break.

Afterward, he ordered brandy for himself and Kate chose Cointreau. What followed was in no way planned. The hotel lounge was rather full and they could not talk easily without being overheard. Kate had poured out the frustrations of a lifetime but had never mentioned Paul or any other man. She had talked about her wish to travel; and about her love of music, which had been encouraged when she was a schoolgirl, because her mother thought playing the piano socially desirable, but which had become another weapon to be used against her. She had much more to tell, Richard knew. He hadn't heard how she had acquired the wedding ring.

"We can't talk here," he said. "Let's go up to your room."

Kate did not give it a thought as Richard ordered more liqueurs and carried the glasses up. She saw him every day; she was used to him. It was the doctor, not the man, whose suggestion she accepted, but it was the man who made it.

Both of them just let it happen. One thing led to another, Richard thought afterward, not for some time examining his real motive in going to Risely at all. There were two armchairs in her room, and he sat watching her as she told him how she had bought the wedding ring in a junk shop in another town and how she wondered about the original owner, whether she had been happy, why the ring was sold. Her face, often earnest when she discussed patients' problems, now showed a variety of ex-

21

pressions, one after the other. When he prompted her with a question, her lips, usually set firmly, rather primly together, were parted. Her eyes were large, dark, and beautiful.

What would it be like to kiss that soft-looking mouth?

He stood up, and Kate, thinking he meant to leave, rose, too. He took his glasses off and put them in his pocket, and she wondered why, but then he moved toward her and took her by the arms, turning her to face him. They were exactly the same height.

"Kate," he said, and when he had kissed her once, found he wanted to continue.

Kate showed surprise, but no dismay. It took gentleness and skill to overcome her inhibitions, but he had both. There was one moment of clarity when Kate thought, coldly, This may be my only chance; and after that there was no going back.

Richard did not leave her that night, except very briefly while he dressed and went down to the reception desk to book a room. If anyone wanted him at home, they would not find him there; it was a chance he must take; he must also make some attempt to protect Kate's reputation. He went quickly back to her; she must not be allowed to feel remorse, or any shame.

3

When the spare wheel had been fitted to Sandra King's Fiat, Gary lowered the jack. The tire sagged.

"Oh, hell!" Sandra exclaimed.

"Got a pump?" asked Gary.

She hadn't, and nor had he.

"Well, you'll get along all right on that. There should be a garage before too long," Gary said. "I'll follow, to make sure you're O.K. Right?"

"Oh, don't bother. There's one in Risely. That woman who stopped was going to The Black Swan there, and she said so," said Sandra.

"I'll follow, all the same," said Gary. "It's on my way. And how about us eating together afterwards?" He'd have to pay quite a bit, with this one, but she looked worth it. They could even go to The Black Swan, if it looked intimate enough.

"It's too early to eat," said Sandra, getting into her car.

Gary followed her to the service station and drove past. Ten minutes later, when she left, his white Escort slid in once more behind her, and he followed her home to Wattleton. She was amused rather than annoyed; she hadn't, in fact, given a straight refusal to his invitation. She wouldn't accept, though, if it were to be repeated.

She lived in a flat in a block on the outskirts of the town and was a market researcher. Gary parked his car in the courtyard of the flats, in the slot next to hers, went into the building with her, and accompanied her up the stairs.

"I need a wash," he said, showing her his hands. "I got dirty in your service, fair lady."

Sandra laughed.

"Well, that's true," she said. "Come in and have a drink."

She never doubted her ability to manage him. She met all sorts of men in her job and was used to the direct approach and the indirect, the flirtatious and the lewd. She was married to an engineer who was at present in the Shetlands, working on an oil-rig project, and not due back until next Thursday.

"The bathroom's on the right," she said, opening the door of the flat and leading the way inside.

Gary had drunk two double whiskies before he met Sandra. Now, after he had washed and tidied himself in her bathroom and had a good look at all the toilet things displayed on the shelves and in the cupboard, he had joined her in the living room and was prowling around, sherry glass in hand. He examined the prints on the walls, the books shelved beside the fireplace, and looked through some of the records stacked under the record player.

"Fond of music, are you?"

"Yes. My husband is, even more," said Sandra. "He used to play the cello."

"I like folk," proffered Gary. He could see nothing remotely to his taste among the available records, so he wandered on to look at an oil painting which showed a solitary pine, some distant mountains, and a foreground of misty green: a Scottish scene. Sandra's husband had liked it and bought it on one of his trips to the north. "What a miserable sort of place," Gary said.

"It's not. It's lovely. So quiet and peaceful," said Sandra.

Gary refilled his glass from the sherry bottle, which Sandra had left on the table. She had run out of beer and it was all she had to offer; he had already had two glassfuls. Now he sprawled among the bright cushions on the cream-colored sofa and patted the space beside him, inviting her to join him.

Sandra took no notice.

"Come on. Be friendly," said Gary.

"Hadn't you better be going?" said Sandra, looking at her watch.

Gary ignored the remark.

"What's wrong? Don't you fancy me?" he asked.

"Don't be silly," said Sandra. "I'm a married woman and I don't sit on sofas with people."

"Married chicks are the best," said Gary.

"Well, you find another one," said Sandra. "Look, I'm grateful for your help with the car but you must go now. My husband will be home soon."

She got up from her own chair and took a step toward the door.

"He won't," said Gary. "He's away till next Thursday. It says so on your telephone pad. Why don't we make use of the time? Fancy leaving a nice little dolly like you all alone. You must miss it, don't you?" While roving round the room, Gary had noticed the entries "J away" and "J back" in red felt pen on the desk diary by the telephone. He stood up, too. "J," he said. "What does it stand for? John? Jim?"

25

"Jeremy is coming home tonight. He rang up," said Sandra quickly, not yet alarmed. Gary had already told her he was a publisher. He was well-spoken and his appearance was good; he was also very conceited and was trying it on—that was all.

Gary filled his glass again. He crossed the room and filled hers, set the bottle down, and stood in front of her, grinning into her face. The smell of liquor on his breath was strong and she realized he must have been drinking earlier. To avoid the close contact, she took a step back and found the arm of the chair in which she had been sitting pressing against her thighs.

"What sort of books do you publish?" she asked. If she could get the conversation back on to an impersonal level, he'd soon realize it wasn't any good and give up.

"Reference books. Encyclopedias. Classy stuff," said Gary. "Improve your self-awareness and your general knowledge. Give your youngsters the start in life that is their right with our twenty-four-part series, bought in easy stages. No commitment. Pity I left my case in the car, I might have sold you a set. I've samples."

He moved toward her, and now she couldn't get away from the chair because he blocked her path. He drank his sherry at a gulp and put down the glass without taking his eyes off her. As he leaned forward, her knees gave and she sat on the arm of the chair. His jacket was undone and she became aware of his urgent state; for the first time she felt a stab of fear. But he'd cool down; she must not panic.

"Let me get up, please," she said.

Gary did not move his body, but he put a hand under her chin and tilted it up. Sandra's knees were tight together as she still tried to keep calm. Of course she could talk her way out of this; it was ridiculous. She was leaning back; if she did not take care, she would topple over into the chair.

26

Gripping her face firmly, Gary applied his mouth to hers. He was very strong. Because Sandra was concentrating on keeping her position on the arm of the chair, her own arms supporting her on either side, he succeeded in forcing her lips apart. She felt his knee against her legs, trying to get between them. Her neck, bent back, felt as if it would snap.

Gary caught her by the shoulders and pulled her to her feet, kissing her again, though to Sandra it felt as if she were being devoured. At last he took his invading mouth away.

"Don't be silly," he said. "It'll be fun. No one's to know. Only you and me."

This can't be happening, Sandra thought, struggling now, turning her head away. She could not get out of his grasp and she could feel his body thrusting against her. At what point did one scream? Surely he would give up when he saw she meant to resist.

But now he had a hand on her breast and was holding her with the other. He was so strong, and she was very small. Wriggle as she might, Sandra could not get free. He moved his hand to her chin again, forcing her head back. She tried to bring up her knee, and at that he moved her backward, forcing her to retreat until she fell on the sofa. Now she struggled really hard, trying to turn her head away and to kick, but he was big and heavy on top of her; his shoulder thrust against her chin, so that her head was still forced backward.

She thought, as he tore at her clothing, that he would have to let go to undo his trousers, but he had her pinned down by sheer weight. This can't be happening, she kept thinking.

Gary still expected her to yield, in the tiny part of his mind that retained the power to think. Others had resisted him before, but in the end he had felt the struggling hands and arms tighten round him. Except once. That time he had held the girl down, as he was holding Sandra now. She had cried afterward and he had said he was sorry. She had not screamed, though.

But Sandra did, at last.

"Don't be silly," Gary said again, this time curtly. "Shut up," and he covered her mouth with a hand.

The face so close to Sandra's looked foolish rather than threatening. She went on making sounds in her throat, her eyes rolling round frantically. But there was no pulling back for Gary now. Breathing heavily, he held her though she still struggled; she freed a hand and pounded at him, but he did not feel her blows; then she scratched his face and he released her mouth for a moment. Sandra screamed again, very loudly, and went on screaming.

Gary grabbed a cushion from behind her and thrust it over her face. He had to stop the noise.

"That'll shut you up," he said, leaning on it. It hid those rolling eyes as well. He reached down to concentrate on what was now so urgent.

Quite suddenly, she went limp.

"There, you wanted it all along, didn't you?" he grunted. They always did. Playing hard to get, pretending to be virtuous. That other one hadn't complained for long, afterward. But Sandra didn't make it easy for him, all the same.

When he had finished and lay panting, spread on top of her, it was some minutes before he realized that she was quite silent now, and had not moved at all.

Gary left the flat an hour later. He met no one as he walked quickly from the building and got into his car, and he did not stop until he had driven right through the town and into the country. Then he pulled in to a side road and slumped over the steering wheel. He began to weep, whimpering cries of terror. Soon he felt sick, and stumbled out onto the grass at the side of the road. Up came the sherry, and then sour-tasting bile. He hung forward over the ditch, shivering and trembling.

He had not believed, at first, that she was dead: faking, more likely, because she'd given in after all. He had patted her face, gently to begin with and then harder, and talked to her pleadingly, then with rising panic. Her eyes were staring at him, but he knew she did not see him; her face was livid. He had never seen anyone dead before.

"But I didn't mean to hurt you," he'd kept repeating, foolishly.

After a while he had pulled himself together. He'd left Sandra exactly as she lay, not even pulling down her skirt, for now he could not bear to touch her, but he went round the flat removing every trace of his identity. He washed and dried the sherry glasses, wearing rubber gloves which he found in the kitchen. Still in the gloves, he wiped the sherry bottle, and then he polished every surface he had touched with the thoroughness of a dedicated housewife. He remembered to comb his hair before leaving, in case anyone saw him, though they had met no one as they entered the building. Some scratches marked his face and he had washed them, dabbing at them with TCP, which he found in the bathroom cupboard. He'd taken the rubber gloves away with him and put them in the trunk of his car until he could dispose of them.

Before leaving, he had smashed up the spruce living room, pulling out drawers and throwing the contents around to make it look as though someone had broken into the flat. The police would think the girl had disturbed the thief.

Someone might have noticed his car outside. He had better get rid of it, since he must continue with his job as though nothing had happened. First thing in the morning he would sell it, and as far away from here as possible. Then there would be nothing to connect him with the dead girl. No one had seen them together. There was nothing to fear. It would simply be another unsolved killing.

He began to feel a little better and stood straighter, breathing in the air. It was fresh and clean, and then he became aware of the country sounds around him: faint rustles in the grass, the squeak of some wild animal.

He got back into his car. He need not panic. She wouldn't be found until her husband came home the following Thursday. He was sure she'd been lying about him coming home tonight. Gary decided he had plenty of time to get rid of the car and settle back to his routine before then.

Hours later, as he was threading his way round the outskirts of Exeter, Gary remembered the woman who had been helping the girl change the wheel of her car when he arrived.

She was dangerous: she could recognize him.

He would have to find her and make quite sure that she didn't.

Gary sold his Ford Escort at a used-car market in the morning. He bought a yellow Vauxhall, transferring all his business books and equipment from one to the other.

"Don't forget your gloves," said the salesman, handing him the rubber pair he had taken from the dead girl's flat.

"Oh—thanks," said Gary, and added, "I keep them in case I have to change a wheel—must keep clean in my job."

The salesman was not interested. He would make a good profit on the Ford Escort and just hoped it wasn't hot. The sooner the deal was through the better, so that he could get on with finding a new owner for the Escort. It was being turned in for an older one, with a higher mileage on the clock, and some cash; sales usually went the other way.

Gary spent the afternoon in a betting shop and lost twenty pounds. He booked in at a pub for the night and in the bar that evening suggested that he had been touring the West Country for the past week.

Lying in bed that night, he thought about the woman who could connect him with the dead girl. She had offered to send help from some place where there was a garage; she was going to a hotel there, the girl had said. Gary would *have* to find her before the girl's body was discovered.

It did not cross his mind that the girl's husband might telephone her, but that was what happened, and when he continually got no reply, he got worried. When Sandra did not answer on Friday night, Jeremy thought she might have been late getting home or stopped to see a friend. He tried several times on Saturday, but then it was probable she had gone out for the day. She might have tried to ring him before leaving and not been able to get hold of him; that could happen when he was on a job. He tried again on Sunday, waiting until ten in case she was sleeping in, then trying again at intervals. She might have gone to visit her mother, who wasn't on the telephone.

By midnight on Sunday he was really worrying, but still trying to explain his worries away. He had tried ringing the Ogdens, a couple who lived in the flat opposite theirs, but had got no reply from them. Sandra might have had an accident. Though she would have something on her to give her own address, there would be no lead to him in Scotland, if she was unconscious.

On Monday morning early he called her once more, and when there was still no response, he tried the Ogdens again. Bill Ogden answered, and while Jeremy held the line Bill went across the landing and rang the bell of the Kings' flat. There was no reply. Jean Ogden looked out the window and saw Sandra's little Fiat parked below in the yard where the residents and guests left

31

their cars. A low wall, about a foot high, separated it from the road.

"She must be all right," Bill told Jeremy. "No accident. Her car's here. Maybe she's staying with a friend."

But if she'd done that, or was visiting her mother, she'd have taken the car. Unless it had refused to start.

Clutching at this straw, Jeremy finally telephoned the police.

4

In his yellow Vauxhall, Gary drove into Risely on Sunday afternoon. The Black Swan, close to the river's edge, was the only hotel, and when he saw it he remembered the name.

He must not be obvious. If anyone saw him near the woman, and then she had an accident or disappeared, they might mention it. He must locate her, wait until she was alone, then follow her. Once he saw her, he would recognize her; he had a dim recollection of someone tall and fair—no chicken, but rather smart. His attention had been on the girl, with those long slim legs. He had not even noticed what sort of car the older woman had been driving.

There was no hurry. He must remember that, and keep his cool. She might take a walk beside the river and then it would be easy.

He parked opposite the hotel, pretended to read one of his books, and, from behind it, observed the comings and goings. At that hour there were few; most of the people on bargain weekend breaks, including Kate, had already left for home.

33

At seven o'clock he decided to chance it and went into the bar. One old man was drinking a pint in the corner. There was no one else there. Gary ordered a Scotch from the pretty blonde behind the counter.

"Thanks, love," he said. "Not busy, are you?"

"No," she answered. Silly question; it was obvious.

"I've come up from Exeter," Gary told her. "Got an important meeting tomorrow."

He had, on any doorstep with any housewife. And he must return to the Grange Residential Hotel in Wattleton, where he lived, as soon as possible, though the management there, in the shape of Mrs. Fitzgibbon, knew that he sometimes stayed away overnight—on business, she supposed.

"Oh," said the girl, not interested.

"Had lots of folk staying for the weekend?" Gary asked.

"Quite a few."

Gary could not ask about a tall, middle-aged woman with fair hair; such an inquiry might stick in the girl's mind. He must use some other approach. There were registers in all hotels. He finished his drink and went out to the cloakroom, looking around on the way. Those books usually stood on tables or counters, handy for people checking in.

An office led off the hall, with a hatch connecting the two. The glass partition was open and, looking in, Gary saw that the room was empty. There was a bell to summon attention. Gary put his head through the hatch and saw the register on a table below the opening. In a few seconds he had taken the register out and was looking at the latest entries. If challenged, he'd bluff, saying an aunt had stayed there recently and he'd wondered when it was.

But such improvisation wasn't necessary. He had time to jot down the names and addresses of three women who had signed in on Friday and to replace the book, then saunter on and out the door of the hotel undiscovered.

One of the three must be the woman he had to silence. Unless she was just a casual dinner guest at the hotel, and he could not bear to think of that.

Meeting at the Health Centre after their first night together had not been difficult for Kate and Richard. There was all the usual bustle protectively around them, with Nurse Meadows dressing minor injuries and syringing ears, and the patients waiting for their appointments. There were forms to complete, the telephone to answer, letters to type. Kate went to and fro in her white coat, her hair by now limp and straight again, although Richard, looking at her closely, thought there was still a radiance about her. To Kate, he seemed once more the kind but slightly abstracted man she had known for years, who never spared himself where a patient was concerned and whom she liked and respected; what had happened seemed, by Monday, unbelievable. It would never occur again.

He sought her out when she was alone in the office.

"All right?" he asked, and as his face showed the tender concern she had seen on Saturday, she felt once more the sensation she had known for the first time that night, as though her bones were dissolving. She smiled at him, and he thought how rarely, in fact, she did smile unless it was in a brisk, cheering way to rally anxious patients.

"I'm fine," she said, and then added, "I may not be, though," looking suddenly mischievous, and her expression reminded him of how Mrs. Havant had so surprisingly looked at one moment.

"Well, you'll tell me, then," he said, thinking, God, what have I let myself in for? How could I have been so reckless?

But she was all right.

At that time, Richard thought he had no intention of repeating what had happened. Kate had not asked why he was in Risely and seemed to think it mere coincidence. But as the date drew near for his next conference in Birmingham, he realized how easy it would be for them to meet again. He need only telephone Cynthia to say he had been delayed. He had a little battle with his conscience; he loved Cynthia, their son, and their family life together. Cynthia's response to him was always warm, her body delightfully familiar. When he was tired, busy, or worried, she understood and was undemanding of his time and attention. She had grown used to the emergency calls which prevented him from going with her to various engagements, or which plucked him away when they were out or even just enjoying an evening at home, and she had learned to fill her life with interests of her own, unresentfully. She was, by now, thoroughly known, totally predictable, and Kate was not.

As others have discovered, *Il n'y a que le premier pas qui coûte*. Richard's meetings were monthly; Kate's weekends were every two or three months. After that first time, Richard was often late back from Birmingham, so that when he stayed away occasionally it did not seem surprising.

Richard had never before been unfaithful to Cynthia. For one thing, there wasn't much time for it in the life of a busy general practitioner, and for another, the few temptations that came his way were easy to resist: he had too much to lose. Who could have imagined that after all these years it would be Kate who changed that? But she was so safe. Cynthia would never know. She had once said, and she wasn't joking, that if she ever caught him cheating her she'd walk out at once, taking Philip with her. She was only thirty-two when she had said this; he wondered wryly if now, ten years later, she felt the same.

Kate's reasons for continuing what had begun in such a random manner were straightforward. She had never imagined such physical bliss could exist, and she wanted to experience it again.

36

It might even improve with practice, and now she belonged to the sexual élite that formed most of the populace, whom she thought she would never join. She knew by now that she would never marry, but this relationship was manageable and safe. It was just astonishing that Richard—so ordinary, bald, looking rather dull, and a lot older than herself—should be capable of transformation into such an ardent, tender lover.

"My lover," she would say aloud, driving up to Risely. "I'm going to meet my lover," and she would marvel at the wonder of it. She looked at married couples now with new insight; unlikely alliances that seemed to prosper could be explained by the magic of sex. It had nothing, necessarily, to do with being beautiful.

The moral aspects of their affair did not worry Kate apart from the minor point that in a sense she was Richard's patient, although to be strictly accurate she was on Dr. Wetherbee's list. Richard had said to her that when Dr. Wetherbee retired, which would be soon, she must move to Paul's list, not his own. Sometimes, in Richard's arms, she tried pretending he was Paul, but it did not work.

Neither Kate nor Richard could have sustained a more demanding clandestine relationship because of the claims of their domestic lives. Kate knew that Richard's first loyalty was to his family, but she understood that by this time he might be bored with Cynthia, whose main interests were cookery, bridge, and gros point, at all of which she was extremely skilled; with Kate he often talked shop, and they worried together about dying patients, the problems of others, and the tragedies. Richard acknowledged the darker side of life with Kate in a way he never did at home.

Gradually, Kate began to stand up for herself more and to pursue her own interests. She left her mother alone while she went to the cinema, to concerts at the Town Hall, or out to

37

dinner. At these times she insisted that Mrs. Wilson have her supper in bed, and in a bowl of soup would be two crushed Mogadon tablets.

Dr. Wetherbee and his wife often asked her to dinner, and sometimes Richard and Cynthia were there, too; Kate would sit demurely in her place and wonder what Richard felt at seeing her and Cynthia together. She went less often to their house. Cynthia, saying to Richard, "It's time we asked poor Kate round," would once or twice a year invite her when there was some other lame duck to be entertained, such as the bachelor vicar with his passion for madrigals. Kate knew perfectly well that Cynthia regarded her as a target for benevolence; she would sit at the gleaming mahogany table watching Richard carve, and she would remember the soft, fine hairs that grew on his arms, now covered by his sober jacket, and the stronger curling mat on his chest and belly. If you only knew, she would think, noting that Cynthia was really quite fifteen pounds too heavy.

She grew steadily more confident.

"If I didn't know it was impossible, I'd think that Kate had found a man at last," Dr. Wetherbee once said to his wife. "At least she's stopped carrying a torch for Paul."

But she hadn't, totally.

On their weekends together, after Richard left her, Kate usually drove into Wattleton, fourteen miles away, and looked around the shops, which were better than those at home. She knew them well and had a favorite café where she went for coffee, and another where she lunched. Sometimes she visited a cinema or a historic house on Saturday afternoons. She never minded Richard's departure. Once, when Cynthia and Philip were both away, he had stayed a second night. They had walked in the hills

38

and stopped at a country pub for beer and sandwiches. Mrs. Havant had borrowed stout shoes, slacks, and a parka from Kate Wilson for the day. With Kate's two personalities fusing, she and Richard had slid into a deeper intimacy and had parted, that time, with real regret; they had not been anxious to put their emotions to such prolonged exposure again, for neither was prepared to play for higher stakes.

Richard had urged Kate to put her mother in The Gables, a comfortable home for the elderly on the edge of Ferringham; many older patients from the practice went there in the end. But Kate wanted to keep the house. She wanted the freedom the sale of it would one day bring her, and her mother's little capital; these would be recompense for all the humiliations she had undergone. She could not explain this, even to Richard; she was not proud of such sentiments.

"It's too late," she had answered. "I can't leave her now."

She should have left while she was young enough to make a career for herself, and it still wasn't too late for that, but she would have to be very strongly motivated to succeed, and Richard knew that Kate lacked that sort of ambition.

"I'd miss you," he said.

"Well, I'm not going," said Kate.

Richard could not have found a mistress more different from his assured, plump, and pretty wife; angular Kate was a challenge and he was proud of his ability to please her. When he stayed overnight at Risely, he left straight after breakfast on Saturday, reaching home in time for morning coffee. He would bound into the house, greet Cynthia very fondly, be ready for whatever the day held, and make passionate love that night. Cynthia would tease him and say it did him good to get away from her, he returned so eager. His was a happy family life.

Mrs. Wilson, however, was always irritated when Kate returned from her short breaks looking rested. The girl's existence was a perpetual reproach; why should Lawrence, who would have been so perfect, have died, and then this pale creature come into being so long afterward, to usurp his place? She was a permanent reminder of something Mrs. Wilson would rather have forgotten; truly, in her book, the sins of the father were visited upon the child.

This weekend was no different. When Kate returned on Sunday evening, her mother, as usual, sent her running up and down stairs on errands devised as punishment because she had been away enjoying herself. Mrs. Wilson asked for sherry, which she did not really want, but she knew that Kate had not replaced the bottle just finished, so there was a perfect opportunity to put her in the wrong. Then her spectacles needed cleaning; after that she wanted part of the Sunday paper read aloud. In fact, she could read it perfectly well herself, she spent a lot of her time reading. However, she had found a particularly dull article about a political figure of very little interest which would be boring for Kate to plod through. She did not bother to listen as Kate read on with her own mind wandering; it was all part of their cold war.

"I need new vests," said Mrs. Wilson when this engagement ended with no outright winner. "Mine have worn thin. You'll have to get them from French's."

French was the company which had bought Kate's father's drapery store to add to its chain. Now remodeled and enlarged, it embraced all sorts of wares, but Kate never went there without a pang of nostalgia. She could remember when the customer's money was screwed into small wooden drums and sent by overhead wire to the cashier in her glass box in the center of the shop, a junction for the overhead railway linking every counter.

"I'll go on Tuesday," Kate said. After a weekend away there was household shopping to be done the next day; she fitted in shopping and changing the library books with getting her mother's lunch. "You'll have to manage with a tray."

She'd have lunch out herself, after getting the undershirts; now that Richard paid for her weekend breaks, she had money for such rare treats.

5

Police Constable Timothy Berry was sent from Wattleton Central Police Station to find out why Sandra King answered neither the telephone nor the door. Most of the flats in the block were empty when he arrived, soon after eight o'clock, for the tenants were mainly couples, both of whom worked. But Mrs. Bradshaw, an elderly woman on the top floor, had seen his car from her window and watched over the stairwell as he rang the bell of the Kings' flat on the second floor.

When he got no answer, she called down to him.

"Mrs. King must be in, Officer. Her car's outside." She knew that Sandra sometimes worked irregular hours, for she watched most of the comings and goings from the flats. Limping, because she had severe arthritis, she came down the stairs. "Can I help?"

Berry sighed. The bright eyes and eager voice indicated a bored woman glad of diversion; but she might be useful.

"Is there a caretaker? Someone with a key?" he asked.

There was not. There was, however, a fire escape at the rear of the building.

"Thank you, madam," said Berry, adding firmly, "I'll come up if I need more help."

He climbed the fire escape and looked in at the windows of Flat 6. He could not see Sandra's body, but he saw the disorder in the room. It was not necessary to break in; the kitchen window was on the latch and he climbed through.

Very soon, Mrs. Bradshaw saw another police car and several more policemen arrive, and then a third car, bearing no official markings, from which stepped a burly man of about forty in plainclothes. When this man, Detective Inspector Bailey, later came to ask her if she had seen Sandra King return to the building, or anyone calling at the flat over the weekend, Mrs. Bradshaw had to reply that she had not. But she had been to the cinema on Friday afternoon, to the five-o'clock showing, and Sandra's car was in its usual spot when she returned at about eight.

"It was there all weekend," Mrs. Bradshaw told Bailey. "I'm sure of that. I didn't go out again, myself."

It was all they had, until forensic came up with something and the doctor gave the time of death, which at first glance he said must have been at least twenty-four hours before the body was found, and probably a good deal longer.

Bailey returned to the flat below and looked down at the suffused face of the dead girl, and the cushions which surrounded her. Gary had thrown down the one he had used among the rest.

"I hope you haven't walked all over the evidence, Berry," said Bailey, moving back himself.

"No, sir. I just made sure that she was dead," said Berry woodenly. He had seen dead girls before in his police career, but he still felt shocked. "There's no sign of a break-in. She must have let him in. Though he could have got in through the kitchen window, as I did. But I had to move her plants and things off the sill first. It's not likely he'd have put them all back if he'd done that."

Bailey agreed. "He'd not have left the window on the latch again, either," he said. "Not with all this mess here. It doesn't match up. He's done this to make it look like thieving. I doubt if there's anything missing. Where's the husband?"

"In the Shetland Islands," Berry said.

"Get him back at once," said Bailey.

He looked down at the girl again. She was in her early twenties, at a guess, and had once been pretty. He saw the platinum ring and little diamond cluster on her left hand; the nails were varnished in a dull strawberry shade, and he bent to look more closely at the hand. One long nail was broken.

"It was the husband who called us because she wasn't answering her door or phone," said Berry.

"I hope he can prove that he was in the Shetlands when she was killed," said Bailey.

Jeremy King flew back. He had been told only that his wife was dead, and he had received the news too late to catch the first plane out of Lerwick, so that he did not reach Heathrow until four-fifteen in the afternoon. By the time he got to Wattleton, Sandra's body had been examined by the pathologist. He was shown her sheeted form in the mortuary, only her face exposed, eyes now decently closed. It was like looking at a caricature of the warm and vital girl to whom he had been married for four years.

"But what happened? How can she be dead?" he had already asked, and now he learned the truth.

"She was raped, you mean," he said. "She resisted, and got killed for it."

"Perhaps." Detective Inspector Bailey's tone was neutral.

"Well, of course she resisted. It's obvious," said Jeremy.

44

"She must have let the man into the flat. It may have been someone she knew. Now, who might she be on intimate terms with, Mr. King?"

"Like that, no one," said Jeremy. "What are you insinuating?"

"Can you be certain? Remember, you were away—gone for several days. You often left her on her own."

"Yes. I have to, in my job. She understands that. We don't—didn't—like it, but there it is. Was." Jeremy banged on Bailey's desk and added furiously, "Good God, Inspector, you don't imagine every wife who's left alone now and then goes having it off with the nearest fellow, do you?"

"The nearest fellow. That would be Mr. Ogden from the flat across the landing, the gentleman you phoned this morning," said Bailey.

"Inspector, Bill and Jean Ogden are our friends," said Jeremy, trying to speak calmly. "We're neighbors. That's all."

"But Mrs. King would let Mr. Ogden into the flat?"

"Of course she would. What are you getting at? Are you implying that Sandra and Bill were having an affair and Bill killed her? Come on, Inspector! That won't do."

"Not that he killed her, necessarily, no, Mr. King," said Bailey. "Tell me again what you were doing on Friday night?"

Jeremy soon realized that he was suspected of coming home unexpectedly to find Sandra and Bill together.

"You mean you really think I could have killed Sandra and then faked a robbery?" Jeremy, incredulous, had not known it was possible to feel such total despair. "Wouldn't I be more likely to kill Bill than Sandra? And would I have rung Bill up this morning?"

"You might have arrived after the man, whoever he was, had gone, Mr. King," said Bailey. "We must explore every possibility."

45

"It's a long way from the Shetlands, Inspector," said Jeremy curtly.

"I'm sure you'll have no difficulty in proving you were there all weekend," said Bailey. "Meanwhile, Mr. and Mrs. Ogden have offered you accommodation for the night. I'm afraid we can't let you return to your own flat until we've finished examining it. Now, would you mind telling me when you left for Scotland?"

It was after midnight before Jeremy was allowed to leave the police station. The Ogdens were still up, waiting for him.

Jeremy did not reveal to them the drift of the police questions.

Of course Sandra had not been having an affair.

Gary Browne studied the three names and addresses he had scrawled on an old envelope: Mrs. Foster in Hammersmith; Mrs. McBride from Fotherhurst, Kent; and Mrs. Havant from Chodbury St. Mary, Gloucestershire.

He ruled out Mrs. Havant immediately because he had met the girl, and the woman helping her, on the southern approach to Risely; Gloucestershire lay to the west and anyone from there would come a different way.

He would try London first, and if he drew a blank there he would go on to Kent. But he must not panic. There was time to act as if everything were normal, and so he spent Sunday night at the Grange Residential Hotel, in his small square room with the one high window, the light oak wardrobe and the chest to match, and the bed with an eau-de-Nil candlewick spread and faded green quilt. In the morning he exchanged cordial greetings with those of his fellow residents who spoke; the silent ones, as usual, he ignored. All ate their sausage and bacon hastily before hurrying off: all were representatives of various firms.

Gary's particular brief was to ring doorbells and tell mothers that if they wanted the best for their children they could give them a head start on their fellows by buying his encyclopedia set: two volumes on trial, a down payment after two weeks, and the other volumes following at monthly intervals. By half past nine he was drinking coffee with a pretty blonde not much older than Sandra King. A small boy playing nearby with his Matchbox cars ignored them both as Gary extolled the merits of the series. The young woman was easily snared and signed for a set.

After that he called on her neighbor; Monday was a good day to find women at home doing their chores. He had a successful, even pleasant time, and Friday night seemed like some bad dream. In the afternoon he pursued several inquiries that had come to his firm by mail, in answer to circular letters sent to addresses taken from voters' lists, and then he set off for London.

It was getting dark as he arrived; he had trouble finding Mrs. Foster's Hammersmith address without a street guide, and spent some time driving round the one-way system only to find himself back at the point where his search had begun. The passers-by whom he asked for directions either gave confusing instructions or did not know the area either. At last he found it: a block of flats much bigger than the one in Wattleton where the nightmare had begun.

He parked the car in the street and studied the numbers over various entrances. He had to walk right round the block and through an archway before he found Mrs. Foster at 151.

It was eight-fifteen when he rang her bell, and she had just switched on the television to watch *Panorama*. Through the spyhole in her door, Mrs. Foster, a civil servant employed by the Ministry of Health and Social Security, saw a young man with brown hair. She did not recognize him and spoke through the closed door.

"Who is it?" she asked.

47

"Good evening, Mrs. Foster," Gary began. "I've been asked to call on you personally to show you a way to enrich your life."

"You're selling something," said Mrs. Foster.

"World-Wide Encyclopaedias," said Gary smartly. "Allow me to show you an introductory volume."

His job certainly made it easy for him to ring bells and get talking without having to think of some other excuse.

"Not interested," said Mrs. Foster flatly. "Good evening," and she went away from the door. The television sound grew fainter as she closed an inner door. Gary had not seen her at all, and he could tell nothing from the voice. What now?

He went down the concrete stairway and stood at the bottom wondering what he could do. Hang about until she emerged from the building? That might mean not only all night but several days. Maybe she didn't work; she had looked well-off. He was still puzzling when a young couple, arms entwined, came in from the courtyard and moved toward the stairs. They were laughing and flushed, eager to get into their own flat quickly, and barely glanced at Gary as he stood there.

"Oh—excuse me—could you tell me, does Mrs. Foster live here?" he improvised. "I thought she was in one five two, but there's no reply."

"Sorry—I don't know anyone of that name," said the man.

"Mrs.—er—Lily Foster," Gary elaborated, using his mother's name. "A tall lady—smart—fair-haired. About forty. She's a friend of my aunt's and I promised to look her up."

Kate would not have liked the extra year added to her age.

"Well, there's a couple in one five two," said the girl helpfully. "They're younger than that and she's dark. Then there's that man in one five three, bit of a creep. I've seen him going in late at night rather the worse, you know." She giggled.

She was a bit the worse herself, Gary thought censoriously: he didn't care to see women that way. He waited.

"We're in one five five," the girl went on. "Oh, what about the one below us—one five one—she's a bit of a tartar—complained when we had a party. I walk about in bare feet now not to give offense. But she's not tall—smaller than me, with hair like steel wool." She giggled again. "Who else is there, Murray?"

Murray racked his brains while Gary stood impatiently. He had his answer now and he wanted to be off, but he must arouse no suspicions; he must hear them out.

Murray remembered a man who played the violin; he'd seen him with his instrument, must belong to an orchestra; and there was a Persian doctor. They couldn't remember seeing a tall blond woman, smartly dressed, on their staircase.

"The porter could help you," said the girl. "He'll have a list."

"Thanks. I'll ask him," Gary said.

They went on upstairs and he hurried from the building. Lucky he'd thought that up so fast; his wits had rescued him from many a scrape in the past and they'd protect him this time, though this was worse than any former trouble he'd been in.

He did not hear the girl he'd been speaking to saying to her husband, "Funny guy. Why was he wearing gloves?" Nor did he see the evening paper which carried a small paragraph reporting:

Mrs. Sandra King, 26, has been found dead in her flat at Albany House, Wattleton, and police are treating the case as murder. Mrs. King is believed to have died of suffocation following sexual assault. Her husband, Jeremy King, 30, is helping with enquiries.

49

6

Mrs. Foster from Hammersmith was the wrong woman, so Mrs. McBride in Kent must be his target, Gary decided, and as he drove out of London that night he began to plan.

She'd be a widow. He'd met plenty of them since he'd been on this door-to-door lark. Businesswise, they were a waste of his time, but they were sometimes interested in other things than what he had, officially, to sell.

The reason that Mrs. McBride must be a widow was because she had stayed alone at The Black Swan. Of course, she could be divorced, but if so, why hide away in such a quiet spot? In his experience, divorcées were either fun-loving and sought the bright lights, sometimes rather feverishly, or they were aggrieved, chasing maintenance payments. The second sort wouldn't stay at The Black Swan.

He stopped at an all-night garage for petrol and bought a flashlight.

Fotherhurst proved to be a small town; the only address Gary had found in the hotel register was The Wigwam, with no street name. He consulted a telephone directory in a booth and discovered that The Wigwam was in Dover Road, the main street running through the town. He found it easily: a shop selling children's clothes. Above, drawn curtains indicated a flat; on one side was a chemist, and on the other a butcher's shop.

Gary sat in his car on the opposite side of the road and pondered. Obviously, Mrs. McBride lived above the shop. He had expected an ordinary house, probably a bungalow, named for some whimsical reason; maybe it looked like a tepee. He had hoped it would be detached so that he could easily approach unseen; he'd do what he'd done to the girl—not the sex bit, of course, but the rest. A pillow, then pull everything out of the drawers. He didn't like having to do it, but he must. Killing the girl had been an accident, but it was her own fault: she'd turned him on right away, showing all that leg; then she'd invited him in and played hard to get. It wouldn't have meant anything, and she'd be alive now if she hadn't been so stupid. Now Mrs. McBride had to die, too. He'd look around when it was done: no good staging a robbery and leaving the day's takings behind; it looked as if it might be a profitable little business.

He could not get in through the front unless he broke open the door of the shop, and that was asking for trouble. The street was deserted now, but anyone might drive past and catch him in the act. There must be a way in at the back.

He left the car a few hundred yards down the road, put on his gloves, and, with his torch in his pocket, went down the nearest side road until he reached a narrow lane which joined it at right angles, parallel to the main street. The footpath was bordered by a row of small terraced houses. Every so often an alley led between them to serve the back doors of several. He'd have to calculate how far from the side road The Wigwam was, to decide which of these houses backed on to it.

51

He returned to the main street and paced the distance from the shop to the corner. Three hundred and seventy-two strides. Two cars passed him as he strode along. Then he walked down the side road again and into the lane. A bicycle without lights went quietly by, and gave him a fright. Three hundred and seventy-two strides down the lane brought him within ten feet of an alley entrance. He looked about. All was quiet, though there was no way to tell if anyone was watching him from a window. He slipped into the alley and found it led round to the left. He'd have to chance the torch: it showed him a concrete path going past the block of houses with, on the right, a row of gardens. If he struck across the nearest, he should emerge opposite The Wigwam.

Gary plunged through a bed of cabbages, the soil soft under his thin shoes, and came to a wire fence. He crossed it and stood in long grass, very wet. A quick flick of the torch showed a brick wall beyond it, about six feet high. He paused. There were familiar urban noises around him: a cat squalled, distant traffic went by. He walked slowly along the wall looking for a spot where it might be climbed. In one corner the branch of a tree on the far side hung over; by clinging to it, he might manage.

It wasn't easy; Gary was no athlete, but somehow he hauled himself onto the top, then swung round and lowered himself until he could drop to the ground. He landed in a heap of garden rubbish. For some minutes he stayed there, panting, partly from exertion and partly from fright. Then, using the torch but shielding the light with his hand, Gary walked gingerly over the garden. It was quite small, and he soon reached the back of the building. He shined the torch round. There was a shed at right angles to the house, and a dustbin stood against it: a rain-water barrel on concrete blocks occupied a corner. Gary cautiously opened the shed; the door squeaked slightly but there was no other sound. He shined the torch in, and saw boxes full of bottles and a stack of empty cardboard cartons. He inspected them. Johnson's Baby Powder, he read, and Dettol. He was in the garden behind the chemist's.

He tried to put himself mentally back in the street outside The Wigwam. Surely the chemist was on the left? The gardens were divided, he soon saw, by a high fence, but by climbing onto the water barrel he reached the roof of the shed and dropped down into the next back yard. His foot caught against a stray object and there was a clatter as something metal spun away from him. He crouched, waiting for discovery, but nothing happened. There was another shed in this yard, and a considerable clutter: boxes, flowerpots, and wire littered the ground. He opened this shed, even more carefully than the other one, and saw garden tools and seeds.

An upstairs window was open. Standing on the shed roof, Gary reached it easily. The curtains were not drawn fully across and he shined the torch, still shielded partly by his hand, between them. It showed a bed, with a large humped mound of bedclothes. A very large hump. Gary looked: two heads, very definitely, showed on the pillow, and as he watched a gentle snore sounded.

He withdrew fast, heart thumping. If this was Mrs. McBride's flat, she'd got some fellow with her; more likely, he'd made a mistake and The Wigwam was, in fact, on the other side of the chemist's.

Cursing under his breath, Gary went back the way he had come, into the first garden. Now he could not use the shed to cross the boundary, but the dividing fence on this side was not high; it was made of interwoven panels and he climbed over easily. In the next garden there seemed to be more space, and his torch showed no shed. A brick wall faced him, and a black-painted door. Beside it there was a small window of frosted glass, its half-light open.

Gary looked round for something to stand on. By reaching in, he might be able to open the larger pane; if not, he must break the glass. There was a dustbin here, too, and he tipped it up to stand it upside down; the contents, tumbling out neatly wrapped in plastic bags, indicated a fastidious user. Standing on this, Gary was able to open the window, but getting through the available space wasn't easy. His foot caught against the lavatory bowl and there was a dull sound, loud to him, though in fact quite faint. He opened the door and let himself out into a narrow passage which, his torch showed, ran the length of the building. At the end, beside a steep staircase, there was a door to the right, bolted from this side. Gary drew the bolt and looked in. He was behind the counter of a shop full of children's clothes; this was, at last, the right place. He withdrew quickly: if there was anyone in the street outside, he would be visible. With the stealth with which he had crept in and out of his parents' house in Nottingham many years before, Gary tiptoed up the carpeted stairs; one tread creaked, and he paused for a full minute before continuing, but nothing happened.

At the top there were several doors. He tried one and found a living room; another, at the back, was the kitchen. The bathroom would be above the lavatory through which he had entered, so Mrs. McBride must be asleep in the room in front.

Gary gently turned the handle and pushed the door open. It rubbed faintly against the carpet. He could see nothing. Covering the torch again with his gloved fingers, allowing only a pencil ray to escape, he shined it on the floor and made out the bed; its foot was toward him, and a pink frilled valance showed up in the faint light. Gary let it creep up over the bed.

At that moment Mrs. McBride woke up, and by doing so saved her life: for one horrified moment Gary beheld snow-white hair

54

and a healthy red face: Mrs. McBride, in her long-sleeved night-dress, was the wrong woman.

He was down the stairs before she could scream, and through the door that led into the shop in seconds. The glass-paned outer shop door was bolted and chained, and even when these defenses were undone it still did not open, for Mrs. McBride was very careful and kept her keys, her final safeguard, upstairs.

Gary looked round wildly, saw a chair, seized it, and flung it at the big plate-glass window, which shattered with a tremendous crash. He stepped through the jagged hole and tore up the street to where he had left his car, and was roaring out of the town by the time Mrs. McBride, who had never in fact screamed at all, was speaking to the police, and before the first lights and the first curious heads looked out to see what all the noise was about.

7

Sandra's photograph was on the front page of nearly all Tuesday's papers. She might have been noticed with her killer, and an appeal for anyone who had seen her on Friday evening was included in the reports of her death. Most of the papers mentioned that her husband had spent several hours helping the police the night before.

Jeremy had found the Ogdens' company almost unbearable. He had been unable to carry on any sort of rational conversation; round and round in his mind went Detective Inspector Bailey's remarks, and he found himself staring with horrified suspicion at Bill, who had a small cut on his face. After a sleepless few hours in the Ogdens' spare bedroom, he went back to the police station.

"What are you doing?" he demanded as soon as he was shown into Bailey's office. "Are you really trying to find this man? Surely someone must have seen him?"

"We're pursuing our inquiries, Mr. King," said Bailey. "It all takes time."

The man's calmness enraged Jeremy.

"My wife was alive. Now she's dead. I want whoever killed her found," he said.

"So do I, Mr. King," said Bailey. "And he will be. Leave things to us. We've had some reports from the lab. There were skin fragments under Mrs. King's fingernails. She may have marked the man, whoever he was."

"So you've stopped suspecting me?"

Bailey said, "Women's scratches at such times aren't always resistance signals, Mr. King. But I'm expecting to hear from the Shetland Islands shortly. That will tidy things up."

Jeremy knew that no one could say for certain where he was during Friday night and early Saturday morning: he had felt a cold coming on and had gone to bed early. However, from so remote a spot it shouldn't be hard to prove that he had caught no plane. As if Sandra's death were not enough to bear without being suspected of having caused it.

Bailey relented, but not much.

"You've a lot to go through, Mr. King, before we get to the end of this," he said in gentler tones. "Who knows what we may not turn up?"

Bailey believed that Sandra had had a lover, Jeremy thought. But if so, why was she killed? Had they quarreled? It was ridiculous to think like that; of course she'd had no lover.

Jeremy could not just hang around in the Ogdens' empty flat all day. He asked Bailey if he might go to see his parents, who lived about fifty miles away, and was given permission. Like some kid, he thought angrily.

The constable taking Bill Ogden's statement the previous day had noticed the scratch on his face, and written it in his report. It would be simple to establish whether the traces of skin and blood found under Sandra's nails were his. There were hairs, too, on the sofa—hairs that did not belong to Sandra, who was dark. These were brown hairs of a paler shade. Ogden and King were both brown-haired; theirs could be matched against the samples and accounted for innocently; a third type would need explanation.

Gary saw the newspapers on Tuesday morning. He got back from his trip to Kent too late to enter the Grange Residential Hotel without rousing the proprietress, so he spent what was left of the night dozing in the car. But he managed to slip in when the door was unlocked and reach his room without being seen; there was always one guest or another who had to be on the road early, before the official hour for breakfast. Gary was in a filthy condition after his nocturnal expedition: there was mud on his shoes, his clothing was torn, and his hands were cut. He cleaned himself up and bundled the suit he had been wearing into the back of his wardrobe. He was now obliged to wear his tan safari jacket and deeper brown slacks, an outfit in which he felt more himself than in his only business suit, but which was frowned on by the firm, who liked its representatives to look conventional.

Somehow he sat through breakfast with his fellow residents, though he had little appetite for the kippers supplied that morning by Mrs. Fitzgibbon. It was in Mr. Perkins's *Daily Mirror*—the front page turned toward Gary while Mr. Perkins, a traveler in furnishing fabrics, was reading the back—that Gary saw the girl's happy, smiling face under the banner headline "DID YOU SEE HER?"

He hurried out of the dining room without finishing his meal, sprang into his car, and raced down the road to the nearest newsagent's, where he had to wait several minutes for his turn to be served and had time to see the photograph, with varying comments, reproduced in the different papers on the counter.

Back in the car, he read one version of the story, learning his victim's name and how her body had been found so soon.

He should have had days in hand to find Mrs. Havant, but by now she'd have seen the paper, too. At this very minute she might be calling the police. Fumbling clumsily with the pages, Gary consulted a map for the route to Chodbury St. Mary in Gloucestershire. He had difficulty in finding the place; it was a small dot some ten miles west of Gloucester itself.

As he drove through the outskirts of Wattleton, Gary tried to rationalize his fears. Even if Mrs. Havant described him to the police, it proved nothing. She hadn't seen him enter the flat with the girl; she'd just left the two of them by the roadside. In fact, she'd probably think nothing of it and not bother; people didn't want to get involved. But he couldn't depend on that. She might already be helping the police to fix up one of those fancy pictures they made, saying, "Yes, that's him," as the features were assembled.

The village of Chodbury St. Mary was a long, sprawling place, with about five hundred inhabitants, a pub, and a Norman church. There were various cottages and houses, a general store and a post office, and several farms. Hill Farm was the address Mrs. Havant had given. Gary supposed all sorts of people ran farms, including elegant widows. Mrs. Havant must pay some man to do the real work, looking after the cows and plowing; such a man might be about the place, posing a serious problem for what Gary had in mind. He didn't like this rushed plan, but now he dared not wait.

At the end of the village street he saw a finger-board pointing up a track: "Hill Farm Nurseries," it read. That meant plants, not cows, which was a relief. He'd ring the bell and see what happened. If Mrs. Havant answered the door herself, and was alone, he'd start on his encyclopedia patter and then act surprised at seeing her. Small world, he'd say. If she referred to Sandra King, he'd say yes, wasn't it dreadful, and he'd left her himself as soon as the spare wheel was on. He'd have to allay any fears she might have and get her away on her own somewhere; he could even suggest they should go to the police together; she might fall for that. Then it would be easy. He'd slipped a large spanner into his pocket. If anyone else was around, he'd act nonchalant and find some way to get her alone. In fact—confidence grew as ideas came—he might get away with bluffing it out, telling her he'd already been to the police and so there was no need for her to bother. That way, he'd learn if she'd already done it. He wouldn't trust her, of course, whatever she said, but it would give him time to think of something.

Hill Farm Nurseries lay bathed in early spring sunlight as Gary drove up the narrow drive to the old stone house, past several large glasshouses and beds of young trees and plants. He saw one distant figure working in a field, but whoever it was appeared not to notice his arrival. Gary was glad, amid so much space with only grass and greenery around, to be safely inside his car with the comforting noise of the engine to protect him from rural silence.

He turned the car before parking in front of the house, in case he needed to leave in a hurry, and he left the key in the ignition. Then he walked up to the front door, one hand in his pocket gripping the spanner, the other clasping Volume I of the encyclopedia series.

He rang the bell.

The woman who opened it was short and sturdy, dressed in a print overall, with a handkerchief tied over her hair.

"Yes?" she said, in unwelcoming tones. She'd had the mop out, doing the kitchen floor, when the bell rang and had had to walk over her clean tiles to get to the door.

"Is Mrs. Havant in?" Gary asked, wearing his best smile. He might have known there'd be a help in a place this size; they were always hard to get past. He met a few when following up postal inquiries for the series. "I think she might be interested in a new guide to knowledge I'm offering on special terms to early subscribers." He brandished his sample volume.

"Mrs. Havant? There's no Mrs. Havant here," said the woman.

"This is Hill Farm, Chodbury St. Mary?"

"That's right."

"But I've been asked to call here specially to see Mrs. Havant," Gary said.

"Someone's been having you on," said the woman. "There's no one here by that name. Good morning," and she moved to close the door.

"But—" said Gary, to a solid block of oak.

He had to accept it. He got into his car and drove fast down the drive, sending clouds of dust flying behind him, back to the village. He would go to the pub and inquire. Besides, he needed a drink after that; wound up for action, his pulse still raced and his mouth was dry with the anticlimax.

Over a pint, he asked the landlord about Hill Farm Nurseries. He was passing through, he said, and had seen the sign. Was it a big place and did it sell roses? He was wanting some rose trees for his mother. Roses were the only flowers he could think of, offhand, by name.

"They do have roses, yes," said the landlord. "Jack Davenport

61

goes in more for vegetables and fruit, though, and he does a bit of herbaceous. Roses are very specialized, with all these new sorts."

Gary nodded.

"Davenport, eh? That's the owner?"

"Yes."

"Been here long?"

"Oh—ten years or more. Doing well now, with all these freezers and everyone buying pick-them-yourself stuff. Has a stall in the market, too, on Wednesdays."

Gary had a second pint and left. When he'd gone, another man in the bar remarked that April was late to buy rosebushes.

"You can get anything now, all through the year," said the landlord. "They ball the roots. Pack 'em in sacking and such."

Laughing, both men forgot about their caller.

When Betty Davenport came in from the greenhouse where she had spent the morning, Mrs. Hughes, her daily help, reported the visitor.

"Asking for a Mrs. Havant, he was. Selling some sort of books."

"How peculiar," said Betty calmly. "I wonder how he got hold of the address."

"Well, I hope it's all right. You can't be too careful, you know. Supposing I hadn't been here, and you out working. He might have helped himself to all your bits and pieces." The house was always left open, and Mrs. Hughes, a keen watcher of television programs, worried. "I wonder if you should tell the police? He might be doing the area," she said.

"Oh, I expect he was genuine," said Betty. "Just got the wrong address."

Mrs. Hughes was not satisfied and went grumbling off, wishing she'd taken note of his car number. Betty was thoughtful, too. Someone had found Kate out at last: the wife, obviously, and had put a private detective on to her. Betty had willingly helped in

Kate's deception; that wicked old woman had ruined her daughter's life, and it was only fair that she should snatch some pleasure. But now what would happen?

She'd have to be warned, for eventually the detective would find her. He'd only got to follow her home, the next time.

Gary was near panic when he left the pub in Chodbury St. Mary. How could he find Mrs. Havant now? Surely he couldn't have made a mistake over the address? But perhaps, in his haste, he'd copied it from the wrong line in the hotel register, or got the name of the house wrong.

Passing the post office, he stopped. If there was anyone by the name of Havant in the village, they would know. He had to wait while an old lady collected her pension and a young one bought stamps for her television license.

The postmistress, a plump woman with iron-gray hair cut in a fringe, and a kindly disposition, told him there was no one named Havant in the village.

"You could try looking in the telephone directory," she suggested. "Maybe it's one of the other Chodburys you want. There's Upper and Lower, over beyond, as well as St. Mary. That's if your friend's on the phone."

"Thanks. I'll try that," Gary answered.

But there were no Havants at all in the directory he found in the telephone box outside. He'd have to go back to The Black Swan and check. And he'd have to make a proper plan for when he found her, too. If she had been at Hill Farm, what would he have done when the door was opened by the cleaning woman? He couldn't have used the spanner, with a witness there, and he might have had a lot of difficulty getting Mrs. Havant out of the house, however much soft talking he'd done. He'd have had to kill the cleaning woman, too, for otherwise she'd lead the police straight to him if Mrs. Havant was found murdered. Gary shuddered at the implications of all this. In a way he was thankful his journey had been in vain. To pick up a weapon and strike a deliberate blow was different from stuffing a cushion over a screaming girl's mouth to silence her.

Of course, he reminded himself, Mrs. Havant wouldn't be suspecting him of having killed Sandra. He must remember that. She would only be able to say she had seen them together, and even if the police questioned him they could not prove he had gone home with Sandra. They'd met no one as they entered the apartment block, and he'd removed every trace of his presence from her flat; that was certain. There couldn't be a fingerprint anywhere.

But they could have been seen from a window.

In that case, the police would already have a description of him and they wouldn't be appealing for help from the public. Or if they were, they'd already have printed one of those photofit shots.

The next step was to return to The Black Swan and have another look at the register.

Over their lunch of cold ham and salad with cheese and pickles, Betty Davenport discussed the morning's caller with Jack and said she must ring Kate up to warn her.

Jack, a burly man with a lined, weather-beaten face and very blue eyes, was in a hurry to get back to his work, packing up the boxes to take to market next day.

"Why not leave her in peace, poor girl?" he said. "She'll hear soon enough, when the fellow does find her, which he will."

"Well, she ought to tell him—her bloke, I mean." Betty found it hard to describe Kate's lover by that term. Why was there no male equivalent of mistress? "It won't be any fun for either of them if he gets a summons."

"It's not a summons, it's a petition," Jack said. "Four dozen, I think."

"Four dozen what? Oh, cauliflower boxes. All right. But to go back to Kate—"

"Leave it till this evening," Jack advised. By then the plants would be loaded and ready for an early start. "She won't be able to talk about it while she's at work. You can have a good natter later. Maybe she'll really come and see us soon. She made a good job of thinning out the lettuce last time."

"Anyone can do that," said Betty. She thought his attitude callous; if he had no sympathy for Kate, he might at least have some for the man involved.

"No, they can't. Some we've paid to help us have overdone it—pulled too many out and disturbed the roots of what they've left, not to mention trampling on everything in sight," Jack said.

"She'll be coming a lot if they've really been caught," said Betty. "The chap'll chuck her—you wait and see—try to save his marriage."

"Will he?"

"Of course he will. He knows Kate can't leave her mother now. Besides, he can't want to marry her or he'd have done it by this time, before Mrs. Wilson got so dependent. Though she's always been that, but she's worse now, since real decrepitude must be catching up on all her pretense. No, Kate's bloke's on to a good thing," said Betty. "Got his bread buttered on both sides. I knew she'd get hurt in the end. Poor Kate. I wonder who he is?"

Gary checked his assets. He had spent pounds on petrol in the last few days, but he had used his credit card to pay for some of it. He could fake his expenses to reclaim most of it in the next few weeks. He still had the balance from the sale of the Escort, which he had taken in cash and not a check, a wise provision as now ready money was not a problem. He could pay for a room at The Black Swan.

He arrived in the afternoon, and as he signed the register had time to read the entry several lines above. He'd made no mistake. "Mrs. K. Havant, Hill Farm, Chodbury St. Mary, Glos.," he read, written in a neat hand.

He would be paying out ten or twelve pounds for the room quite needlessly, but he was too perplexed to extricate himself now. He signed, accepted the key to Room 32, and carried his briefcase up to it. Once inside, he pulled off his tie and flung himself down on the bed. There, exhausted, he fell into a sudden deep sleep and woke only when the maid, wishing to turn down the bed, tapped on the door. Because she heard no answer to her knock, she came in and, seeing Gary stretched out on top of the covers, was about to withdraw.

"Sorry, sir," she said automatically. Guests got their beds turned down if their rooms were vacant; if it wasn't convenient when she came, too bad.

"No—it's all right." Gary was trying to surface from the depths of unconsciousness into which he had fallen. The hotel was not very large; this chambermaid might have come across Mrs. Havant. "I've been traveling all day—and most of the night," he said, with perfect truth. "Down from Scotland," he elaborated. "Quite worn out, I was. I didn't mean to fall asleep like that."

The maid, a middle-aged woman who lived in the village and wanted to get home as soon as she could, nevertheless smiled at him; he seemed a pleasant young chap, sitting there in his pale yellow shirt with his hair on end like a bit of a kid; terrible hours some of these fellows had to put in, she knew.

"Nice place, this. Aunt of mine stays here sometimes," he tried. "Mrs. Havant. Know her?"

"Oh, we all know Mrs. Havant," said the woman, smiling all the more. "One of our regulars—been coming for years. A very nice lady. And Mr. Stearne, too. Very pleasant, both of them."

The relationship between Richard and Kate had long been obvious to the hotel staff, and now they were automatically given adjoining rooms, which simplified things. Richard never used his professional title when signing in.

Gary had the presence of mind to hide his surprise at this revelation.

"Yes, he is nice," he agreed.

This remark allayed the maid's sudden fear that she had, perhaps, been indiscreet. Gary stood up so that she could turn down the bed, and when that was done she went away, still smiling.

Gary was hot, sticky, thirsty, and very hungry. He had eaten no solid food since breakfast, and he had left most of that. He'd have to pay for the room so he'd use it. He had a bath and shaved; he kept a battery-powered razor in his briefcase, but he had no spare clothes with him so the yellow shirt had to go on again, the gaudy Y-fronts, and the yellow socks. Then he went down to the bar. He'd have to find Mrs. Havant through this Mr. Stearne, whoever he might be.

He'd missed the radio news, but there was an evening paper in the bar and he glanced at it. There was a small paragraph about the murder. The police, he learned, had received numerous calls from people who thought they had seen the dead girl, but they were still anxious to hear from anyone who had not yet come forward.

Gary sauntered along to the reception desk. He'd be leaving early, he said. Could he pay now, as he'd have to go before breakfast.

"I'll pay cash for dinner," he said.

While the receptionist made out the bill, Gary helped himself to the register and, whistling softly in a carefree way, looked at it again. "R. Stearne," he read, a few lines below Mrs. K. Havant's entry, and the address, 53 Windsor Road, Ferringham. It was an easy address to remember.

8

Without complaint, Bill Ogden parted with a strand or two of his hair, and suffered a drop of blood to be drawn from a finger. He was so appalled at what had happened to Sandra King that he would have submitted to any indignity, not just to be exonerated himself but to narrow the field for the police. He and Jean had spent the weekend with friends in the country; he had cut his face while helping his host massacre the brambles in their over-grown garden. If they had been at home, knowing Sandra was alone, they'd have asked her in to lunch on Sunday, or at least for a drink.

"Was she dead by then?" Bill asked. "We might have seen something—heard something—if we'd been at home when it happened.

"You very likely might, Mr. Ogden," said Detective Inspector Bailey.

All morning, telephone calls had been coming in from people alleging they had seen Sandra. Every one must be investigated, although some were clearly from cranks. It needed only one genuine report to provide a lead.

"What about the husband?" Detective Chief Superintendent Hawksworth, in charge of the case, inquired.

"Well, sir, no one seems to have seen him on Friday night, it's true. He says he had a cold and went to bed early, but he couldn't have left the islands without being noticed and it's quite a lengthy journey, back and forth. We're checking, of course, but I'm sure we're looking for someone else."

"Someone she knew. Someone she let in willingly."

"Seems likely."

Thieves, on the whole, didn't go in for rape. The few items of value in the flat were still there, and the disorder created by the killer looked exactly what it was: a haphazard upheaval in the room.

"Her business colleagues? Clients?" Hawksworth asked.

"Frith's going through the statements now," said Bailey.

A detective sergeant and a constable had been sent to Sandra King's firm and everyone there had been questioned; all were asked about her friends and acquaintances. A list of the calls she had made on the day she died had been supplied, so that her movements could be checked. Detective Sergeant Frith and his team of constables would sift this information and follow every line; if she had a lover, his identity might be discovered in this way, but it could be a slow business.

While the two senior officers were talking, a constable came in.

"We've had a call that seems like something, sir," he said. "From a garage—a service station—in Risely. That's about fourteen miles south of here. Seems the deceased called there for air and a couple of gallons of petrol around half past six on Friday evening. The owner served her himself. Clark's the name. He's

70

sure it was the same girl—he remembered the blue Fiat 127, too, though not the number. He's on his way over."

"He would remember the girl. Anyone would. She must have been very pretty," said Detective Chief Superintendent Hawksworth. He felt cold fury at the merciless end of that young life. He was the father of two high-spirited daughters much the age of the dead girl, and was not inclined to Bailey's belief that she might have been a tease and asked for what she got—though not to the point of murder, naturally, Bailey had amended his assertion. Emotion had no place in a police inquiry, however, and Hawksworth added, "She was alone at the service station?"

"Yes, sir."

"Hmm. Well, it's a start. Means we know where she was at half past six on Friday. She must have met the murderer after that," said Hawksworth.

"The girl told him she'd had a puncture and the spare was down," Detective Sergeant Frith reported after interviewing Bert Clark from Risely Service Station. "Checked all her tires, he said, to make sure, before she left."

"She'd changed the wheel herself?" asked Bailey.

"She didn't say otherwise. I asked him," Frith said. "And she went to the toilet to wash."

Bert Clark had not enjoyed his visit to the mortuary. He'd felt sick, looking at Sandra, and had indulged in a flow of invective about nothing being too bad for whoever had done such a thing.

"Give you the come-on, did she?" Frith had asked.

"Me? No—just pleasant, she was. Ordinary, like, but nice."

"See all sorts, don't you, on the pumps?" Frith remarked.

"Right," agreed Clark. He had run the service station for ten

71

years now, with the help of a series of lads and his wife. "Some rum ones, too."

"Get some tarty bits?"

"Oh, yes. If you can judge by looks, that is. Most folk are in a hurry, you know, but some look good for a giggle."

"It's not the right spot, eh?"

"No."

"But this girl wasn't like that? Flighty?" Frith gestured.

"A very nice sort of girl. A respectable sort of girl," said Clark firmly. "Smartly dressed, but nothing flashy."

He was not a young man. His judgment was probably sound, Frith thought.

"Tipped me, too, for doing the tires. Twenty pence," said Clark. "Most don't bother."

"Bet you let most of them get on and do it themselves," said Frith.

"Well, yes." Clark, recovering now from the visit to the mortuary, managed a grin. "Not the pretty ones, though."

Frith was glad that Sandra King's Fiat was already in for testing; he'd get them to go over the spare and the jack, particularly.

Kate usually glanced at the newspaper while she ate a quick lunch in the kitchen, but on Tuesday, because she did not come home after shopping for her mother, she did not see it until the evening. At first she could not think why the girl in the photograph looked familiar.

"The dead girl's small blue Fiat stood outside the block of flats all weekend while her body lay undiscovered," she read.

Blue Fiat. The girl with the puncture.

Mrs. Wilson's bell rang but went unanswered as Kate read, for the second time, the report and its appeal for anyone who had seen the girl to come forward.

"It is believed she was sexually assaulted," said the paper.

As clearly as if he were standing before her now, Kate could picture the face of the man who had stopped to help with the wheel: the brown eyes, set rather close together; the thick brown hair; the confident smile.

If Kate hadn't left them together, it wouldn't have happened. The blood pounded in her ears. He must have gone home with her and—oh, but wait a minute—no, that couldn't be right. The brown-haired man had helped her change the wheel; that was all. She must have met someone else later on. The man who'd helped her, and whom Kate had seen, would account for himself when he read what had happened. It was just the most horrifying coincidence that Kate had seen the girl, and that man with her; that was all.

Her mother rang again, and Kate went upstairs to be scolded for the delay.

"What's the matter with you? Are you ill?" snapped Mrs. Wilson, for even she noticed how white Kate was. "I've been ringing and ringing," she added, falsely, for she had rung only twice.

"I feel a bit sick," said Kate truthfully.

Her mother did not want to hear about that. It was time for Kate to help her undress and put on her dressing gown so that she would be ready for bed whenever she felt like it, after supper and her evening's television.

The old lady went along to the bathroom while Kate folded away the old-fashioned bloomers and the thick stockings, and hung up the warm, button-down dress, so easy to slip on. Then she went down to prepare supper: an omelet, spinach, and potatoes tonight, followed by a fresh pear poached in syrup. All the time she was preparing the meal, the memory of Sandra King never left her mind. She, Kate Wilson, had seen the dead girl with that brown-haired man and it was her duty to say so. The man was not the killer, but even so, the police must be told about him in case he did not come forward himself. They would eliminate him—that was the phrase—from their inquiries. He might be as reluctant as she was to be involved and so, however innocent, keep quiet. It sounded, in fact, as if the husband were suspected of the crime. Round and round in Kate's mind went the few reported facts and her own part in the affair.

She'd find Richard and tell him about it. He'd say it was all right and she need do nothing; that was what she wanted to hear. She'd slip over to his house after her mother was settled. She'd never called there uninvited before, but after all, why shouldn't she? Richard would know at once that she must have an important reason for coming and would make an opportunity for them to be alone, without Cynthia. She'd pretend she'd come about old Mr. Donkin's artificial leg; she'd heard from the hospital about fitting him for a new one only that day—a perfect excuse. Clinging to this plan, she got through the evening's routine and dissolved two Mogadon tablets in the milk drink her mother always took after she got into bed. That would send her to sleep so that Kate could slip out without saying she was going. Mrs. Wilson always slept well, even without drugs; the Mogadon, prescribed for Kate herself, was just to make sure. Kate always kept a good supply.

By nine-thirty her mother was already dozing with the radio on. Kate switched it off and the old lady did not stir. Kate turned out the light. Fifteen minutes later she had parked outside Richard's large neo-Georgian house and was standing in the road.

The house was blazing with lights and a number of cars were parked in the road outside; the driveway was full of cars, too. The Stearnes were having a party. Richard had not mentioned it, but then why should he? Maybe he'd even forgotten that Cynthia had planned one; he left all such things to her.

Kate couldn't disturb him while he had guests. What could he tell her that she did not already know herself? She must get in touch with the police.

But she would have to explain. If she said she was on her way to stay with a friend, they might ask who, and then want to know why she was on that road, since it was not the way to Chodbury St. Mary. They might check up, and Betty would draw the line at lying to the police. Kate drew the line at doing that, too. The police might find out that she had been using a false name; for all she knew, that was an offense itself, but in any case her secret would come out. She'd be made to seem ridiculous and Mrs. Havant's existence would cease. But, worse than that, Cynthia would learn about it; she would have known that Richard was at The Black Swan, for he never left a false address in case he was wanted in an emergency. She would wonder why he had not mentioned that Kate was there masquerading as a widow. Cynthia would never, herself, suspect the truth—Kate had no illusions about Cynthia's poor opinion of her—but his silence would be significant. If their affair was discovered, what would she do? And what about Richard's career?

Too much could be lost. Kate would have to keep quiet. After all, as she'd already decided, the brown-haired man couldn't have killed Sandra King; they must have parted quite soon after Kate left them—twenty minutes, at the most—And he didn't look like a killer.

But what did a killer look like?

Kate got back into the Mini and drove home. She put the car away in the garage and went into the house. As she unlocked the back door, she could hear the telephone ringing, and in her hurry to answer it she flung the key down on the kitchen dresser, with her car keys, leaving the door unlocked.

9

After he had paid his bill at The Black Swan, Gary went back to his room and rumpled the bed to make it look as though he had spent the night there. He left the key on the dressing table. Then he went out to his car and drove off quietly, for he did not want to be noticed.

Two pints of beer at Chodbury St. Mary and another just now at the hotel were all he had consumed since early that morning and he felt light-headed. He'd stop at a fish-and-chip shop on the way to Ferringham and eat as he drove. He had to find the home of this Mr. R. Stearne, though how he would trace Mrs. Havant from there he did not know. There might be an address somewhere—a letter from her. Anyway, there was no other means of finding her that he could think of and, having got away with breaking in once, Gary felt that he might be successful a second time.

He entered the outskirts of Ferringham at nine-fifteen. Nowhere on the way had he seen a fish-and-chip shop, and now he was acutely hungry. He drove slowly through the town; there might be some sort of take-out place open. He did not want to go into a restaurant or café where he might be remembered afterward if there was trouble. The same instinct made him reluctant to ask the way to Windsor Road. Ferringham was too small to be included among the town plans in Gary's road map. The thought that R. Stearne, like Mrs. Havant, might have given a false address occurred to him, sickeningly, for the first time.

He reached the end of the main street, which had the uniform appearance of most towns where old buildings had been refaced with modern shop fronts or demolished to permit whole new blocks to be built. There were the usual supermarkets and stores, with some smaller individual shops among them. There was a little traffic about; some boys on motor bicycles roared past Gary as he drove along and he saw a group of youths gathered outside a pub. The shops thinned out as he reached a district of small, old houses. He saw a telephone box and stopped. He'd check up on R. Stearne.

The box smelled horrible, and most of its windows were cracked. Gary wrinkled his nose in distaste as he turned the tattered pages of the directory and shined his torch on the faded paper. There were only two Stearnes. Stearne, Dr. R. W., 53 Windsor Road, he read. A doctor! That was a surprise. Perhaps Mrs. Havant lived in Ferringham, too. He consulted the entries under "H" but found no one listed with that name. Maybe she worked in the hospital; doctors were busy folk and couldn't have much time to go hunting for bits of skirt. There must be a hospital here, in a place this size, Gary reasoned, and he looked it up. Perhaps Dr. Stearne lived near it; he could ask for directions to the hospital without rousing suspicions; if he inquired for Windsor Road and then left traces of a break-in, he'd be in danger. But the hospital was in Victoria Street; that was no help.

Gary drove on and, coming to some traffic lights, turned left, for the road ahead would take him out of the town. He was now in an area of large, detached houses set back from the road behind hedges or fences, with names like The Firs, Copse Court, and The Leas inscribed on their gates. Thick curtains were drawn across the windows, allowing only an occasional shaft of light to show. This was a prosperous area; Gary had plenty of experience at assessing such things in his work. A doctor might easily live in such a neighborhood.

He stopped at the next turning and read the name of the road: Castle Street. It did not occur to him that Windsor, Victoria, and Castle were related terms and that a town planner might have used them in a single district; he found Windsor Road by accident, driving up and down scrutinizing the names at each crossing.

There were a lot of cars parked outside Dr. R. Stearne's house when he came to it, and all the lights seemed to be on. He drove past slowly and saw the brass plate on the gate. Then he turned at the end of the road and passed the house again. This time he parked behind the last car. He was still very hungry. He must try to form a logical plan, like entering a downstairs room and going methodically through any bureau there might be. Meanwhile, now that he knew where the place was, he could find something to eat and return later, when everyone had gone to bed.

He was sitting in his car, well away from the light cast by the nearest street lamp, when Kate drove up in her Mini. He saw the small car stop on the opposite side of the road, and he saw a tall woman emerge from it and stand on the pavement, looking across at the doctor's house. She had straight fair hair and wore a beige raincoat. It took Gary some seconds to realize that he was looking at Mrs. Havant. Kate stood there for quite a time, his prey delivered so unexpectedly to him. Then she got into her car and drove off.

Gary started his own car and followed her, keeping some distance away; there was so little traffic about that he knew he could not lose her.

The telephone went on ringing as Kate hurried into the house. It would not waken her mother, for Kate had had it moved into her own small sitting room so that she could use it in privacy; Richard knew she could talk without being overheard and he rang her sometimes when Cynthia was out.

Confused thoughts rushed through her mind as she hastened to answer it. Could the police have somehow discovered already that she had failed her civic duty, and tracked her down? Wouldn't they be more likely, in that case, to send an actual policeman?

Fearing disaster, but unspecified, she picked up the receiver and said a tense "Hullo?"

"Kate, where have you been? I've tried several times to get you," said Betty Davenport. "I thought you never left your mother alone?"

"Oh, yes, I do, sometimes." Kate was filled with relief at hearing Betty's voice; a true friend. Betty did occasionally call after Kate's illicit weekends to make sure everything had gone off all right.

This time, however, Betty was the bearer of important tidings and, like most messengers of bad news, reluctant to deliver it yet anxious to know its effect.

"It's just that there was this man, Kate, and I thought I'd better tell you," Betty said, her voice blurred by a crackle on the line.

"What man?"

"A man called here this morning asking for Mrs. Havant. Mrs. Hughes—you know, my help—she saw him. She told him there was no Mrs. Havant here. She couldn't understand it."

"But—Betty, who could it be?" Kate's voice rose in alarm.

"Well, I can only think you've been rumbled, Kate. He must have got the name and this address from the hotel, surely? No one else knows about it, do they?"

"No."

"Your fellow, whoever he is—his wife must have got suspicious and put someone to follow him," Betty said. "It's the only explanation. Better go somewhere else next time. Or why not face up to it? You've got nothing to lose and he might marry you."

"That's out of the question," said Kate. "Oh, God!"

"Well, don't panic. You've got a breathing space. Mrs. Hughes told him he'd got the wrong address and he left at once."

"He must have been at the hotel. Watching us," Kate said, appalled.

"Well, not exactly—not in mid-act, as it were," said Betty. "But he must have followed one of you. Your chap, obviously, since the wife must be employing him. But there's nothing to connect you directly, as you gave the wrong address."

"I suppose you're right," said Kate doubtfully.

"I thought private detectives wore shabby raincoats and loitered in doorways—didn't come out in the open," Betty said.

Kate thought so, too.

"It must be a question of definite identification," Betty went on. "Don't worry too much. It's not the end of the world, even if you are found out. Happens all the time."

"But Rich—he's got a good marriage," Kate said.

"You worry about yourself, not him," Betty advised. "There's your mother to be reckoned with, too."

Betty knew that Mrs. Wilson could destroy Kate; indeed, she had gone some way toward doing so already. But Betty did not realize that Mrs. Wilson was capable of casting Kate off altogether; if she discovered the truth about Kate's weekends, her disapproval would be so intense that the house and the money, all Kate's future security, might be willed away in malice to some charity: there was no other surviving relative.

"Marriage has a dark side, Kate," Mrs. Wilson had once said. "Be glad you've been spared all that." She meant, Kate had supposed, sex. Yet she and Kate's father must once have felt love, desire, something.

"I won't be meeting him again," Kate said to Betty now. "Not like that." For of course she would see Richard every day at work.

"Oh, Kate, why not?"

"The risk's too great," said Kate. "It'll have to stop."

"Well, you know best about that, but I think it's a shame," said Betty. "Come and see us, then. Really come, and soon."

"I will," Kate promised. "And thanks, Betty."

It was not Betty's revelation that had made Kate decide it must be ended; she had known it when she stood in the road outside Richard's house where a party of which she had no knowledge was in progress. She had been left out because she was dull and there would already be surplus women guests; there always were at any party. The lively ones would have been asked tonight; Cynthia would entertain the misfits some other time. She was a good and dutiful woman, like the one in the Bible whose price was above rubies, and Richard loved her.

He had told Kate that one could love two women; love wasn't a cake restricted in size; its capacity expanded to enfold an unlimited number of recipients. Parents, he earnestly explained, loved large families of children as much as one or two. It was his nearest approach to describing what he felt for her.

What if it were Paul she had been having this affair with? Kate idly considered, as she had many times before. Paul no longer played rugby, but squash twice a week kept him fit. He was burly now, and still exuberant; his florid face was still handsome. He

81

continued to tease Kate and to invite her out for a beer occasionally. She realized that he no longer had any power to hurt her and she would not mind if she never saw him again.

But she would mind if she never saw Richard, and she was not going to give herself that pain. She was simply going to end the affair before he did, either from fear of discovery or from boredom, or because it had become a burden. When they started it all, he had been the victim of middle-aged wanderlust and she happened to be there, convenient, available, and safe.

Kate knew now that her obsession with Paul had been fantasy; this business with the dead girl was real, and so was the threat of the private detective. Kate must steer herself through the perils threatened by both; the detective, with no further evidence, would give up; the morning papers might reveal that the police had found Sandra King's killer.

It was rather a lot to ask for such satisfactory outcomes to her problems. Kate sat for a long time in her shabby sitting room, thinking about it all.

10

Jeremy King had spent a wretched few hours with his parents, going over and over what had happened.

His father, also an engineer and now retired, was practical.

"You can't really think that Ogden was involved with Sandra," he said.

More emotional, his mother wept and said that Sandra would never have looked at anyone but Jeremy.

"I trusted Sandra, but why should I trust Bill?" said Jeremy. He thought, with shame and remorse, of one night he had spent with a girl who worked for his firm and who was on a project with him. Both had got rather drunk; it had meant nothing to either of them. He had almost forgotten that it had ever happened and the girl had since left the firm. "He might have tried it on," said Jeremy. "Sandra did resist; that was why she was killed."

"Poor dear girl," said Jeremy's father, but he wondered if really she had not been a poor foolish girl. "Do you think she'd have given a lift to someone in her car? A hitchhiker?"

"No, she wouldn't do that," said Jeremy. "We'd talked about it and she'd promised."

"She might have fallen for some hard-luck story," his father theorized, eyes narrowed as he puffed at his pipe.

It was a possibility. People had been attacked and robbed when they stopped to help what looked like accident victims. Sandra might have fallen into such a trap. It was all very well to deplore the fact that no one would help anyone else these days; with the terrible things that happened, it was scarcely safe to step outside one's door, thought Jeremy's mother, looking out the window at a field where some cattle tranquilly grazed. No babies now, she thought sadly: no grandchildren. Her shocked mind could not yet make the imaginative leap ahead to when Jeremy might manage to put the present horror behind him and start to rebuild his personal life.

"The police will get whoever did it," she said. "Someone will have seen him—that awful man—going into your flat. Or leaving."

"The police seem to think I could have done it myself," said Jeremy bitterly. "Come all the way back and killed her, and flown off again. Imagine."

"They always start like that," said his father. "Eliminating the nearest. After all, they didn't know Sandra. They might have thought she was a different sort of girl, and then you would have had cause. For anger, I mean. It's fair enough. They have to think of that."

By midafternoon, Jeremy could stand the inactivity no longer. The police might have discovered something by now, and if he stayed away he wouldn't hear about it. He decided to go back.

"So what have we got?" Detective Inspector Bailey asked Frith, and began to answer his own question. "A young woman is found dead—suffocated—following sexual intercourse. The presence of skin and blood particles under the nails and the posture of the body indicate rape. Also, one nail was broken. A well-turned-out girl like that would have neatened off the torn nail if it had happened earlier."

Frith nodded. Sandra King must have been a well-turned-out girl before her killer had left her lying there, clothes torn, legs apart, like a pathetic rag doll.

"The stomach contents showed she hadn't eaten for several hours," Bailey continued. "But she'd had some sherry just before death. Time of death, between seven and ten on Friday evening; the doctor can't be more precise. No sign of the sherry glass or the bottle from which she'd drunk, so she could have stopped at a pub."

"There was a half-full bottle of sherry in the flat," Frith reminded him. "Wiped completely clean. No prints of any sort—not the dead girl's or her husband's, as you might expect."

"Right," said Bailey. "So her murderer drank a glass of sherry with her and cleaned up. And he didn't feed her, so we'll save some shoe leather checking the restaurants."

"There's some positive info about the car, sir," said Frith. "We already know she had a puncture—she told Clark, at the Risely Service Station. The spare wheel—the damaged one in the boot of the car—is covered in dabs."

"So are the others, I should think," said Bailey. "Wheels get changed around when the car's serviced."

"Yes. But there's a set on the spare—the punctured one, on the rim—that doesn't match most of the others found on the bodywork, only on the tools—the jack and the wheel brace, and the external door handle on the driver's side. Oh, and the boot. The one on the wheel isn't very sharp, but there's a nice one on a hubcap, too."

"So somebody changed the wheel for her?"

"Yes. And then opened her car door for her and closed it after her."

"But he didn't get in with her? None of these mystery prints inside?"

"No."

"But we know she was alive—and alone—after the puncture. She was at the garage getting her tire blown up."

"Yes, sir. But why hasn't the bloke who helped her come forward?"

"May not have heard the appeal—doesn't want to be involved—is driving a long-distance lorry to Turkey. A dozen reasons," said Bailey.

"Maybe he followed her home. Risely's not so far," said Frith, and leaned over to pick up a report from Bailey's desk. "There, sir. Read what the lads had to say about the bathroom at the Kings' flat."

Bailey ran his eye over the relevant page as Frith continued.

"By the time we found her, more than two days after she died, the towels in the bathroom would have dried off, if they'd been recently used. They were very grubby—or one of them was. She didn't look the type to leave dirty towels about. There might be oily deposits on one, if whoever had helped her washed there."

"There might," said Bailey. "And she had a wash at the service station, so although she might have washed again, she'd already have got the worst off."

"Yes. And be more likely to have washed properly before drying, in any case," said Frith. "My wife's always getting at me for wiping half the garden dirt off on the towels. Isn't yours?"

Bailey ignored this observation.

"So she had help, and whoever gave it waited for her near the service station and followed her home— quite possibly by arrangement," he said.

86

"Yes, sir," said Frith, and added, "I've asked the lab to check the towels for oil."

"We'll ask the news boys to appeal for this man, direct," Bailey decided. "If he's just a good Samaritan, maybe he'll come forward. If he doesn't, we'll find him. Someone will have noticed them, wherever it happened. If you see someone changing a wheel by the side of the road, you notice it, don't you?"

"Right," said Frith. "Even in traffic. You have to pull out to avoid them, unless they're in a lay-by. Poor bloke, you think, I'm glad it's not me."

"Well, thanks to the girl's methodical work sheet, we know where she'd been that day," said Bailey. Sandra had meticulously noted her calls down after each was made. The last visit was about fifteen miles south of Risely, where she was making a district survey about a popular product. "So we know which roads were the most likely ones. Get on with it, Frith!" Bailey said, in a sudden roar. "Don't hang about. We want this on the radio news, television, the lot—not just the morning papers. Step on it."

From her flat above the Kings', Mrs. Bradshaw watched the police activity and at last she saw Jeremy return. She did not know that he had been to see his parents and thought he must have spent all day at the police station. Detectives were still working in his flat. Limping heavily, for her hip was very painful today, she went out onto the landing and started down the stairs: she wanted to talk to him. By the time she reached the first floor, however, he had been allowed into his flat to fetch some clothes; he had left the Shetlands without waiting to pack. He emerged at last, carrying a small case.

"Mr. King—could I have a word with you?" Mrs. Bradshaw

87

spoke softly and put out a hand to him. Her glance went to the constable standing at the door of the flat.

"Well—" Jeremy hesitated. What was there to say? Everyone was sorry.

"Perhaps you'd come upstairs for a minute?"

She seemed tense. Jeremy knew she spent hours at her window. Perhaps she had noticed something whose significance the police would not understand.

"Let me just put these things away and then I'll come," he said, fitting the key the Ogdens had given him into their door. "You go on. I'll follow."

He had accepted the Ogdens' insistence that he stay with them until he was allowed back to his own place; a hotel was the alternative, and there he would be at the mercy of the press. The police presence here did offer protection from the persistent reporters.

Mrs. Bradshaw painfully ascended the stairs again. She got out the remains of a half-bottle of brandy and two glasses, then waited for Jeremy to join her.

"I've been thinking so hard about Friday," Mrs. Bradshaw said to Jeremy. "I went out at about three-thirty to meet my friend at the cinema—I caught the bus from the end of the road. We had tea at the cinema first—it's quite nice there." She paused, reflecting. "Your wife's car wasn't outside then, Mr. King. I'd have seen it. There aren't many cars outside during the day when you're all at work. It was there when I got home—getting on for eight, it was, quite late for me these days—and it was there the rest of the weekend. I told the police, of course."

Mrs. Bradshaw hadn't been at her window the one time it mattered, to see Sandra return, Jeremy thought wearily.

"So pretty, she was, and so friendly," Mrs. Bradshaw said sadly. "I loved to see her. She had such a sweet smile. We always had a little chat when we met. It's a terrible thing to have happened." She paused again. "Mr. Ogden's car wasn't there in the evening—I do remember that. They've got a new one; I noticed it the other day. A red one."

They had; a Datsun—and Jean Ogden might have been out shopping in it. The local supermarkets stayed open late on Fridays. Bill could have stayed at home, knowing Sandra was alone in the flat. The Ogdens had not left for their weekend away until Saturday. Bill could have killed Sandra and calmly left the next morning knowing she wouldn't be found for several days.

"There was another car, though," Mrs. Bradshaw was saying. "A white one, parked next to your wife's car. I didn't recognize it. I don't think it can belong to anyone living here, unless it's new. I know most of them."

"A white car?" Jeremy tried to pay attention. He had the feeling he was hearing something important. "You saw a white car you didn't recognize next to Sandra's?"

"Yes."

"And was it there next day? This white one? On Saturday morning? You said you saw Sandra's then."

"No, it wasn't. Or not in the same spot," said Mrs. Bradshaw. "I know that, because the Ogdens' was there, next to your wife's—her blue one and their red one. Then the Ogdens went off early—they were away for the weekend." She blushed slightly, an odd thing to see happen to her lined old face. "You must think me an awful busybody, Mr. King, but I get pleasure from seeing you young folk."

Jeremy said urgently, "This white car, Mrs. Bradshaw. What sort was it? Do you know?"

"No, I don't. Well, it was much the same size as Mr.

Ogden's—a little bigger, perhaps. Different—another make. Quite ordinary."

"You didn't notice anything else about it? Its number?"

"It had some books in the back. I did see that," said Mrs. Bradshaw. "I went past it, coming in. I'm afraid I'm rather naughty and I always clamber over the little boundary wall and walk past the cars instead of coming round to the entrance. It saves quite a walk for me and I can manage that little bit of mountaineering by holding the post in the corner. Your wife usually parks—parked—there, if there was a space. She helped me over, once."

"Yes." Sandra had commented on Mrs. Bradshaw's short cut. "Go on," Jeremy urged. "There were books in the car?"

"Yes. A pile of them, like dictionaries, and a lot of leaflets. It was parked just by the street light, you know. That's one reason why I come in at that spot. I could see them plainly."

Detective Inspector Bailey himself came at once to see Mrs. Bradshaw, and Jeremy was allowed to remain in the room while she repeated what she had told him. He tried to conceal his impatience while she explained again how she climbed over the low wall which divided the tenants' parking area from the pavement outside.

"The car may have belonged to someone visiting one of the flats," Bailey pointed out. "Mr. King, have any of your friends got white cars? They're very common nowadays."

"Several have," said Jeremy.

"So have you, Inspector," said Mrs. Bradshaw. She nodded toward the window. "Yours is just like the one I saw."

Bailey had not come in his own car but in a white police Ford Escort, driven by Frith.

"Well," he said. "Let's try it. Right away."

11

Gary sat in the car outside No. 11 Chestnut Avenue, unable to believe his luck. He'd almost failed to recognize the tall, untidy woman in the shabby raincoat standing outside the doctor's house. He did not wonder what Mrs. Havant was doing in the road when a party was going on inside; he had found her, and that was what mattered. He saw her drive through the gateway of No. 11; then her car vanished as she put it away in the garage, which was screened from the road by shrubs. After a while, some lights came on in the house.

Gary moved his own car farther up the road and turned in to a side street; there was plenty of space to park. Then, on foot, he approached the house and glanced up and down the road. There was no one in sight. Gary slipped between the gateposts and into the cover of a large syringa bush. There he waited for a long time. The lights he had already observed stayed on. It was a large house for someone to live in alone; perhaps, after all, she was married and had given her old man the slip for the weekend.

Moving from bush to bush, Gary worked his way round to the back of the house, and there a patch of bright light shone out, lighting up the flower bed below. The kitchen blind was not drawn. Gary, moving nearer, could see right into the empty room. He saw an old-fashioned dresser with cups hanging from hooks and plates stacked on its shelves. He waited. Mrs. Havant would surely return to turn out the light, and when it was dark he would try to get in. He thought again of food.

He had to wait for a long time before Kate came into the kitchen. She suddenly appeared, approaching the window to turn on a tap at the sink beneath it. Gary stared at her. Could this really be Mrs. Havant, so plain, young-looking, with straight fair hair hanging in limp fashion on either side of her face as she bent forward? Then she frowned. She had frowned like that before deciding to leave him with the girl. Gary knew that clothes and make-up did a lot for a woman; obviously she wasn't bothering now, away from her fancy man. He remembered his sister, in rollers and face-pack, then tarted up to meet some boy; what a difference. He hadn't thought of her for a long time, and he hadn't seen her since he left home a year after his mother died and his father's schoolteacher sister, who did not like Gary, came to keep house.

As he watched, Mrs. Havant suddenly reached up and pulled the blind down across the window, cutting him off. Then a light went on upstairs.

Gary crept toward the back door and tried the latch.

Kate had emerged from her troubled, conflicting thoughts requiring comfort; she had gone to the kitchen to make some tea. Then, as the night was cool and she felt chilled, she decided that a hot-water bottle in her bed might help her to sleep. She took the tea through to her little sitting room, and the bottle upstairs.

While she was doing that, Gary opened the back door and slipped into the house.

Kate put the hot-water bottle in her bed and laid her nightdress on it. Once in bed, hugging the bottle in its woolly jacket and having taken a Mogadon, she would slide into sleep, away from the horror of the murdered girl and the desolation of ending her affair with Richard.

She went into her mother's room. The old lady had turned on her side, a strand of white hair across her cheek, a hand up to her chin, like a child. Her breathing was very soft. Mrs. Wilson looked small and defenseless, and Kate felt ashamed of the impatient dislike she so often felt for her. She wondered about her parents' life together; her father must have found his marriage far from satisfactory. Kate remembered that he often went off on buying trips to factories and warehouses. He might have been going in search of other things as well as merchandise; perhaps her mother knew and hid her humiliation behind the screen of invalidism. Kate's own conception may have been the result of some truce or breach in their separate existence; they had never shared a bedroom within her memory.

She would never know the truth, and at this distance she could not judge. She did know that Cynthia Stearne had told Richard she would divorce him immediately if he were unfaithful; her own mother might have felt the same, but in those days divorce was still regarded as a scandal. To deny freedom to her father, if he had wanted it, may have been the worst punishment her mother could inflict.

Kate went down to her sitting room, where by now the tea had brewed, and turned the radio on. She switched to Radio Two, as the other B.B.C. stations had closed down for the night, and was just finishing her tea when the midnight news came on. There were items about a threatened strike and a rise in the cost of oil. Then the announcer's voice took on a note of restrained urgency.

"Police investigating the death of Mrs. Sandra King, found apparently suffocated in her flat in Wattleton yesterday, are appealing for anyone who saw her on Friday evening to come forward. It has been established that she called at a garage at Risely, fourteen miles south of Wattleton, at about half past six, driving her blue Fiat car. She was alone."

An enormous wave of relief swept over Kate. She had checked in at The Black Swan at twenty minutes past six herself; the brown-haired man could not possibly have had anything to do with Sandra King's death, because she had been seen alone after that. Kate had been panicking needlessly. She got up and picked up her small radio to carry it upstairs, turning the volume down so that it would not wake her mother. She could go to bed now and she would sleep with an easy conscience. She moved toward the sitting-room door while the announcer was describing Sandra and the clothes she had been wearing at the time of her death. Kate, still listening, opened the door.

He stood outside.

As his hand went over her mouth to stop her from screaming, Kate knew that this man, whom she recognized at once, had to be Sandra's killer.

By midnight, Wattleton Central Police Station was still busy. Men had to deal with the drunks, the loiterers, and the traffic offenders while the major inquiry went on, but by that time all the tenants in the Albany House block where Sandra King lived had been asked if they'd had a visitor on Friday night who arrived in a white car, probably a Ford Escort.

There had been several visitors, but none had such a car.

After the late news on radio and television, two telephone calls were received from people who had seen someone changing the wheel of a car not far south of Risely. One thought there were three cars drawn in at the side of the road, a white one and two others. He was not sure now which was the one in trouble. The second caller had noticed a girl at work on a blue car but saw that she already had male help. He could not describe the helper but thought he wore a brown suit.

"Observant, eh?" remarked Detective Chief Superintendent Hawksworth, reading this report. He noted that the local law, in the areas where each of the callers lived, had already been asked to go round and take statements without delay. "So now we're looking for a white car, possibly a Ford Escort, driven by a man in a brown suit. He followed the girl home in his own car, possibly by arrangement, which explains why she was alone at the service station."

"Yes, sir. And he may be a publisher's representative," said Bailey. "The books Mrs. Bradshaw saw in the car."

Both knew what must be done. Publishers' representatives covering the area must be traced and interviewed, and their cars checked out.

"Might be a bookseller," Bailey added.

"Do they tout their wares around like that? I suppose some of them do," said Hawksworth. "Check them, anyway."

But the work could not begin until the next morning when bookshops and offices opened, and the task of tracing all the possible men might take days.

Gary, after entering the house, had heard Kate moving about upstairs and had hidden in a broom cupboard under the stairs. Then he had heard her coming down again, and after a while, faintly, the sound of music. When the news bulletin began, he could not make out the actual words and he had emerged from his hiding place to creep over to the door and listen. Kate opened it before he had got farther than the realization that time was still on his side.

Kate dropped the radio as he grabbed her. It went on playing,

95

lying on the floor. As Gary stood with his hand over Kate's mouth and his other arm round her body, crushing her against him in the mockery of an embrace, both of them heard the announcer report that the dead girl was believed to have changed a wheel on her car sometime on Friday evening, probably on the southern approach road to Risely. Would anyone who either helped her or saw her please get in touch with Wattleton C.I.D.?—and the telephone number followed.

Fearful, heart-stopping shock and terror made Kate incapable of any movement for a few seconds. But she was as tall as Gary, and she had the strength of panic. She twisted her head furiously against the hand that was over her mouth and brought her own hands up against Gary's body, trying to pull away from him. She was a great deal stronger than Sandra King. Gary, also terrified, pushed Kate across the room until her back was against the wall. She still tried to struggle, but in the moments when his hand slipped from her mouth she did not scream. She couldn't; but sounds came from her, gasps and grunts as she fought against him. This was a different sort of struggle; here there was nothing sexual, just animal panic on both sides, and Kate, without understanding what it was, felt Gary's fear beside her own.

Eventually he held her pinned against the wall, his hand across her mouth, his body, legs, and other arm clamped to her so that she could not move.

"Mrs. Havant," he said in a sort of hiss. "I found you, Mrs. Havant."

Astonished eyes stared into his flushed face above the hand that stopped her mouth.

"And you're here alone," he added. It stood to reason. He'd heard no one else moving about while he hid in the cupboard, growing hungrier by the minute and with his stomach rumbling in protest. There had been no sound of voices from upstairs and no one could sleep through the noise they had just made, he was sure. It had drowned the sound of the radio, still playing as it lay on the floor.

In fact, there had been merely thumps, groans, and mumblings. No furniture had been knocked over. The loudest noise was the heavy breathing of the two protagonists.

Slowly, gingerly, Gary took his hand away from Kate's mouth, ready to cuff her immediately if she did scream.

Some power of thought returned to Kate. Her mother, doped with Mogadon, would sleep through all but an extreme noise; she must make this man go on thinking that she was alone or he would go upstairs and kill her mother—that was certain. He meant to kill her—Kate—she knew, but she would make it hard for him.

"My husband will be home soon," she said fiercely.

There was no time now to wonder how this man, knowing that she could identify him, had traced her. He had raped that wretched girl before he killed her, and it seemed to Kate that he must mean to rape her, too.

"You're a widow," Gary said.

"No."

"You are. Dirty weekending with your boyfriend, that doctor. You should be ashamed." Gary turned her round, twisting her arms up brutally behind her back, as he had seen thugs do in films, so that he stood behind her; then, covering her mouth again, he pushed her ahead of him out of the room toward the kitchen. "You're not expecting your husband. You're a widow," he repeated. "There's no one to help you."

Well, that was true enough.

Gary thrust Kate into the kitchen, still holding her arms up behind her back. When she tried to resist, the pain was excruciating, and she had to comply with his kicks and shoves.

Very little money had been spent on the kitchen at No. 11 since Kate's father's death. An old-fashioned clothes airer, used every week, still hung from the ceiling, worked by a pulley on a strong cord. Gary had never seen one before, but the principle was obvious. He pushed Kate along to where she could reach the hook round which the rope was secured and freed her right hand, still holding the left bent up at her back.

"Undo it," he said.

Kate did so, letting the rack come down with a rush, in the hope that the wooden struts might strike his head, but he ducked out of reach, pulling her clear, too. He pushed her against the wall, facing it, his knee against her back, ignoring her flailing right arm while he loosened his tie, pulled it over his head, and then held it between his teeth. He caught her free arm. All this time she had not screamed, and even if she did the nearest houses were too far away for her to be heard, but he had to make certain. He caught both her hands together and slid them through the loop of his tie, pulling it tight. Then, wedging her against the wall with his body, he pulled a handkerchief from his pocket, balled it in his fist, and thrust it into her mouth, forcing it in, almost choking her, holding her nostrils when she would not part her lips. Kate managed to kick him hard on the shin while he did this. She had never felt such blinding rage in her life; it far outran her fear as she shook her head furiously, revolting against the obscene intrusion into her mouth of the soiled cotton fabric.

Gary needed a knife. He had to cut the cord holding the airer and tie her up. Then he could get some food. With a meal inside him, he'd be able to think. She was so bloody tall, much too tall for a woman. He didn't like them big; it did nothing to him.

There would be knives in one of the drawers beside the sink. He forced Kate to move across to it. Clamping her against the

98

sink, her back to him and his body pressed solidly to hers, he opened a drawer, pulled out a large knife, and, holding it to her neck, forced her over to the airer again.

The knife would be plunged into her throat or between her ribs. Kate waited for it to happen, still angry more than frightened, but when she understood that he meant to cut the rope from the airer, she felt amazed relief at the respite.

It was difficult for Gary to cut the cord while he still held Kate, but the knife was very sharp, kept so by Kate's custom of whetting it against the back doorstep, and he managed. Then he forced her into a chair, her arms behind her, and lashed her legs and trunk to the chair. When her hands were securely knotted with cord, he removed his tie from her wrists and replaced it round his neck. Finally he tied a tea towel across her gagged mouth. The two things that occupied her to the exclusion of almost every other thought were the pain in her arms, bent up behind her, and the assault on her mouth.

Gary foraged in the refrigerator and found bacon and eggs. He used Kate's omelet pan to fry them, with a fat slice of bread and a hunk of butter. He spilled fat on the stove and the kitchen grew smoky. Then he sat at the table, shoveling food into his mouth.

Kate stared, amazed. How could he eat when he had killed one woman and was going to kill another? For that must be his intention. Kate, watching while he devoured his meal, thought that perhaps he did not mean to do it here, or why delay? If he took her away from the house, no one would know what had happened until she was found, if she ever was.

He spread butter thickly on several slices of bread, then piled jam on top and munched greedily. He had made tea, not going back to her sitting room for the small pot Kate had used but taking the Crown Derby one from the cupboard; he had stood the milk bottle on the table and found the sugar packet, shoving the wet spoon straight into it. Kate, sometimes slovenly herself, watched in disgust.

Gary, having eaten, felt much better, but he studied his prisoner with increasing dismay. This was no five-foot-two dainty little piece to pick up and dump. She'd take some shifting, and she'd fight, too, if she got the chance. He could knock her out with a blow on the head, he supposed, even kill her here and move the corpse, but the idea of deliberately doing it repelled him. He had not meant to kill Sandra King, only to silence her screams; now, to hide that crime, he had to kill this woman in cold blood. He had thought it would be easy, once he found her, and so it might have been if she had lain asleep and unaware. But faced with the living person, he discovered that it wasn't so simple. He could not strike some sudden fatal blow. He would have to engineer an accident.

He had the knife, a good sharp one: she'd do whatever he dictated, with that against her throat.

While Gary ate his meal in Kate's kitchen, Jeremy King and the Ogdens were still up, discussing Mrs. Bradshaw's information about the white car. Jeremy knew now that on Friday night the Ogdens had gone out to dinner; when they returned at half past eleven, they had left their Datsun in a space beside Sandra's Fiat; the unidentified white car had gone by then. Jeremy felt ashamed of his suspicions about Bill.

"What could those books have been that the old girl saw in the car?" Bill wondered, pouring the last of his whisky into Jeremy's glass. "Would a publisher's representative have them loose? I thought they took them round in suitcases."

"Mrs. Bradshaw said they looked like dictionaries," said Jeremy.

"Could they have been encyclopedias?" asked Jean. "A girl at work had someone round wanting her to buy a set only the other day. You have the first volume or two on trial. They make it sound as if you're denying yourself and your kids a golden chance of advancement if you don't accept."

"Encyclopedias! That might be it," said Jeremy.

He got up and left the room. A different constable was now outside Jeremy's flat; the man agreed at once to mention encyclopedias to Detective Inspector Bailey. Sometimes they were peddled from door to door; a caller had been to see his own wife recently; very persistent he'd been, she said.

Jeremy did not know that this sympathetic officer was Police Constable Timothy Berry, who had found Sandra, and who had certified at her post-mortem that this was, indeed, the girl he had discovered dead.

How much longer would the police keep him out of his flat, Jeremy wanted to know. In fact, he was not sure if he would ever be able to sleep in it again, but he wanted the right to do so.

"Not much longer, Mr. King," said Berry. "There's a lot that can be done, though, you know, that may be useful later. We've new ways with cameras—we can sometimes pick up footprints off carpets, always assuming no one else has trodden around too much after chummy. Then there's the analysis of clothes, and that. Cushions, and so on." He did not refer to the towels now at the lab, where evidence of oil stains was being sought. "Some tiny thing may trap him, when we get him. We may know he's done it, you see, but it's another thing to prove it. A piece of thread off his clothes—we have to be sure it's not off your clothes, say, or someone else rightfully in the flat—a small thing of that

101

sort can be crucial." Berry spared him details of the intimate factors which, in a case like this, could give incontestable proof of identity.

Jeremy was grateful for this explanation from the kindly constable. It was rather different from the attitude the police had adopted toward him at the start of their inquiry. He said so.

"Well, you see, this sort of thing's often a domestic," said Berry. "That's where we always have to begin. Funny things go on in marriage. It takes all sorts."

Jeremy supposed he was right.

Berry's wife, Joyce, was sitting up in bed feeding their month-old daughter when he got home after his stint at the flat. He was due back on duty at eight o'clock the next morning and she had something to say about the excessive hours expected of a policeman.

"You've married a bobby, love. You're stuck with it," he said. "Got to be done, when something big's on."

"This murder?"

He nodded.

Joyce knew that Tim's sensitivity was not yet blunted by experience: she hoped it never would be.

"You'll find whoever did it, and some judge'll say he was sick and couldn't help it," she said.

"He may not have meant to kill the girl," said Berry. "Maybe she screamed and he tried to shut her up. That's possible. He meant the rest of it, all right."

"He raped her, you mean," said Joyce.

"Yes. She could have asked for it, though."

"Led him on, you mean?"

"Yes. But who'll ever know what really happened?"

Over the downy head of their infant daughter, held against her mother's breast, the two young parents looked at one another.

102

Suppose some young chap talked his way in here, into the house, selling something Joyce might find interesting, and was given a cup of tea—then wanted to try it on. It could happen.

"Joyce, love—that bloke selling encyclopedias—remember? You mentioned it the other day. Tell me about him."

"What a change of subject," said Joyce. "You should be thinking of sleep, not encyclopedias. Come to bed."

"I will. Just answer this first, please. It's not a change of subject and I'll explain later," said Tim, adopting the stern, concentrated mien which she seldom saw but which was often his official aspect.

"I said nothing doing. I don't know what firm he came from," said Joyce. "But Madge Billings might, if it's important. I think he sold her a set."

"It could be very important, love. What'd he look like, this guy?"

"Well—ordinary sort of size—not as tall as you—but not small. About five ten, maybe. Very neat. Brown hair and a yellow shirt," said Joyce, trying to visualize her caller. "He had quite a way with him, in fact; I do remember that. They have to, I suppose, calling door to door, to be successful. On commission, aren't they, after all?"

"Sort of bloke you'd ask in and think nothing of it?"

"Oh, yes—if he was selling something I wanted. He was clean—quite nice-looking, really. Hair not too long, yet well styled." She grinned up at Tim, with his short back and sides that looked so good under his flat cap. "Why do you want to know about him?" She sat suddenly more upright in the bed, her movement squashing her daughter's nose against her. "He's not the one, is he? Did he go selling encyclopedias to that girl and—?" Joyce's face showed horror.

"That's leaping ahead a bit, love," said Tim. "We have to have

103

evidence. But I'll just nip round to Madge's now, and see if she's got those books."

"What? In the middle of the night? You can't—they'll be asleep," said Joyce.

"I know," said Berry. "But this is a case of murder. It can't wait till morning."

He stood up, bent to kiss his wife's warm and parted lips, ran a large, gentle finger against the petal-soft cheek of Miss Tessa Berry, and went to the door.

"See you, love," he said.

12

It was after three o'clock on Wednesday morning before Police Constable Timothy Berry got to bed after reporting what Madge Billings had to say about the man selling encyclopedias, and delivering the volume she had taken on trial. Bailey thought it important enough to telephone Detective Chief Superintendent Hawksworth about, even though tracing the salesman covering that area could not begin until the firm's head office opened the next day. But the prints on Madge's volume which were not her own could be matched against those found on the tools and the wheel of Sandra King's car. Madge Billings had given the salesman a cup of coffee while she browsed through the introductory volumes he displayed. He had thick brown hair and brown eyes, and a cut on one cheek. She had not noticed what sort of car he was driving. In the morning, she would come in to build a photofit picture of him; so would Joyce, Berry's wife.

The man would be found and then his brown hair could be matched against the strands found in the dead girl's flat. The hair alone would not be evidence enough, but his blood group would be compared with the scrapings from under her nails. There would be other forensic evidence, if he was the man who had raped her.

Berry had been granted an extra hour before coming on duty in the morning, since he had been up for most of the night.

"Big deal," grumbled Joyce as he sleepily ate his Weetabix and glanced at the paper. He had said very little when he returned home, but this morning he told her that she was never to let anyone into the house whom she did not know or did not expect to call, looking fierce as he said it. Sandra King might or might not have led the killer to make sexual overtures to her. Even if she had, and then changed her mind, that did not lessen his crime. If she hadn't, any woman could have been his victim.

"There's a lot in the paper about the case," Joyce said as her husband read the front page where a fresh picture of Sandra appeared.

The appeal for anyone who had seen her changing a wheel on her car somewhere south of Risely was given prominence. "Police are particularly anxious to trace the driver of a white car, possibly a Ford Escort, believed to have been parked at the scene," he read. The papers had certainly been prompt with their cooperation; this front page must have been altered just before going to press. Berry's attention was caught by another report, lower down on the page.

Police investigating the break-in at a children's-wear shop in Fotherhurst, Kent, have announced that the intruder left clear footprints in the garden at the rear where he made his entry. Mrs. Winifred McBride, 67, a widow, who lives above the shop, woke to find a man in her room on Sunday night. He fled, escaping through the plate-glass window of the shop. Mrs. McBride had just returned from a weekend break at a hotel in Risely,

106

Warwickshire. It is thought the thief may have known of her absence from home and expected the premises to be empty.

Berry read the paragraph twice. The killer of Sandra King had no cause to go to Kent; if he was the encyclopedia salesman, he was touring Wattleton on Monday morning. The fact that Risely cropped up in both cases was a coincidence. But whoever had laid out the page had noticed the coincidence, too, and thought it worth pointing out; otherwise the lesser item would have been on an inner page or not reported at all.

Coincidences of such a nature should be investigated. He would show the paper to Detective Inspector Bailey.

On Wednesday morning at half past nine, Mrs. Burke put her key in the lock of No. 11, opened the door, and almost immediately screamed, but not loudly.

Mrs. Wilson lay on the floor at the rear of the hall. She wore a woolen dressing gown over her brushed-nylon nightdress, and one of her bedroom slippers, little bootees, had come off, exposing a scrawny white foot.

"Oh, my goodness! Oh, dear Lord," cried Mrs. Burke, hurrying forward to her employer, who looked as if she were dead.

But Mrs. Wilson was still breathing, and as Mrs. Burke bent over her, she opened her eyes and groaned. No intelligible speech, however, emerged from her lips. Her face was contorted, her mouth drawn down at one side, and she seemed unable to move.

Mrs. Burke stepped over her and went on into the little sitting room where Kate—so inconveniently, in Mrs. Burke's opinion—had had the telephone moved. She found that the receiver was off the hook, dangling on the end of its flex, and making an angry buzz. Mrs. Burke could obtain no dialing tone as she jiggled the hook up and down.

"Oh, dear," she kept muttering, and finally replaced the receiver while she picked up a cushion to put under Mrs. Wilson's head. Another noise could be heard now that the telephone was silent. Kate's portable radio lay on its side on the floor, and from it came the voice of Pete Murray. Automatically, Mrs. Burke picked it up, switched it off, and put it on a small table. What had got into Kate, leaving it on like that? A tray, with a teacup and saucer, the small brown teapot and jug of milk, was also on the table, but Mrs. Burke barely registered this unusual sight as she hurried back to the hall. Having made Mrs. Wilson look more comfortable, with her dressing gown and nightdress pulled down over her wasted legs and her slipper replaced, Mrs. Burke tried the telephone again. If it still wasn't working, she'd run next door.

But the dial tone had returned and the ambulance was summoned.

Mrs. Burke went straight upstairs and fetched a blanket to cover the old woman. Mrs. Wilson's eyes opened, and she groaned.

"Don't worry, the ambulance will soon be here. We'll have you right in a jiffy," Mrs. Burke assured her, though she felt no such confidence. Why had the old lady come downstairs, so early? On the rare occasions when she felt like making the effort, she waited until Mrs. Burke arrived to support her during the descent, or until Kate came home at lunchtime. Sometimes she liked to snoop around while Kate was out, looking for things to complain about later. Mrs. Burke knew all about it; she often heard Mrs. Wilson recite her grievances.

Now Kate must be told of her mother's accident. Mrs. Burke picked up the telephone to ring the Health Centre. She might as well do that while waiting for the ambulance; perhaps she should have rung there first and asked Dr. Wetherbee to come.

The telephone was not answered straight away, and when it was, a harassed, unknown female voice replied.

"Kate? That isn't you, is it?" Mrs. Burke demanded. "Your mother's had an accident."

"Who is that, please?" asked Nurse Meadows.

Mrs. Burke knew her first remark had not been sensible. She pulled herself together.

"This is Mrs. Burke, Mrs. Wilson's help. I want to speak to Kate—Miss Wilson. Her mother's been took bad," she said.

"Miss Wilson hasn't come in this morning" said Nurse Meadows. "We thought she must be ill. I tried to ring her. There was no reply."

"Well, I can't understand that. Unless she's gone for help. Or perhaps her car broke down. Anyway, her mother's very bad— she's lying here on the floor. I've sent for the ambulance," said Mrs. Burke.

"I'll tell doctor," said Nurse Meadows. "I expect one of them will come."

"Dr. Wetherbee looks after Mrs. Wilson," said Mrs. Burke firmly.

"I'll let him know," promised Sybil Meadows, ringing off. She rang back a few minutes later to say that Dr. Wetherbee was on his way, and to tell the ambulance men, if they arrived before he did.

They did. Mrs. Wilson, they were sure, had had a stroke. They got her onto their stretcher and into the ambulance, well tucked up, and were in favor of driving off with her at once.

"Maybe the doctor will want to keep her here," Mrs. Burke kept saying, for surely Mrs. Wilson would not survive and would want to die in her own bed, as she had always planned? "But where can Kate be?"

That was what Dr. Wetherbee said after he arrived. He agreed with the ambulance men's diagnosis, and gave them permission to be on their way. By now, Mrs. Wilson had relapsed into total unconsciousness and her breathing had grown stertorous.

"Wherever is Kate?" asked the doctor again, when the ambulance had gone. She had never been late for work before.

"I don't know. Perhaps she had an accident on the way," said Mrs. Burke, for by now anything disastrous seemed likely. "She left her wireless on," she added.

"What do you mean?"

Mrs. Burke explained, but Dr. Wetherbee barely listened. He marched on and opened the door that led into the kitchen.

"Good God, what's happened in here?" he exclaimed. "Surely Kate doesn't usually go off leaving the kitchen in this sort of state?"

Mrs. Burke followed him into the room.

"Oh, dear Lord," she said again. "That she doesn't. Kate always washes up her own things. I fetch her mother's tray down the days I come."

The kitchen was in chaos. The wooden clothes airer was on the floor, its supporting cords hacked away so that just the ends remained fixed to the struts, a chair lay on its side; Kate's special omelet pan, full of congealed fat, was on the stove, which itself was covered with spilled fat that had spattered around. A used plate, knife, and fork lay on it askew; a half-full bottle of milk, an open packet of sugar with a spoon stuck in it, and a packet of butter, the wrapping torn, were on the table. So were the Crown Derby teapot and a mug Kate had bought at a West Country pottery on a trip to Paignton.

"Kate never did all this," said Mrs. Burke. "The best teapot, too."

"Don't touch anything," said Dr. Wetherbee in a grim voice. "Let's have a look upstairs."

Mrs. Burke, with a proper sense of what was right, led the way into Mrs. Wilson's room.

110

"No breakfast tray," she said.

Dr. Wetherbee was already heading toward Kate's room, along the passage. Her bed was turned down, the candlewick spread folded and laid across a chair.

Mrs. Burke stepped forward again. She knew Kate's ways. She put a hand under the sheet and drew out the rubber bottle, now cold, and Kate's nightdress.

"Oh, what can have happened to her?" Mrs. Burke exclaimed. "Has she taken leave of her senses?"

"She didn't sleep here. Her mother woke and Kate didn't come, so she got up and went downstairs, perhaps to telephone for help," said Dr. Wetherbee, and Mrs. Burke nodded at these deductions. "She must have felt ill while at the telephone and staggered away from it to the hall. Or she may have fallen near the telephone and crawled towards the door."

"But what can have got into Kate?" Mrs. Burke lamented. "All this mess—and going off at night!" She could only think that Kate had somehow lost her wits, defiled the house, and run away. She would not have been altogether surprised if Mrs. Wilson had finally driven her daughter to some rash deed, but not one of this sort: more a direct act against her mother.

"Kate didn't do this," said Dr. Wetherbee. "At least, I don't think so." It could be a gesture, an appeal for help from one called upon to bear too much, but Dr. Wetherbee thought Kate not a likely subject for such behavior. He could not understand why she, of all people, had been kidnapped, but he felt she must have been—perhaps by mistake, in place of someone else. "I'll ring the police, Mrs. Burke," he said. "While I'm getting through, would you just slip out and see if her car's gone?"

Dr. Wetherbee rang the Health Centre after calling the police. He had to hold on for some time before Nurse Meadows an-

111

swered the telephone and switched him through to Richard, who was seeing a patient.

"I'm at Kate's," said Dr. Wetherbee. "Something very odd seems to have happened here. Kate's disappeared—her bed hasn't been slept in—the kitchen is full of dirty dishes—very unlike Kate, Mrs. Burke says, to leave such a mess—and the old lady's had a stroke. Mrs. Burke found her in the hall."

"Oh, my God!"

The patient, a pale man with symptoms which indicated a duodenal ulcer, stared at the doctor in surprise.

"Kate's car's gone, too," Dr. Wetherbee went on. "She could have had too much of it, I suppose, and snapped—driven off somewhere. But she seemed all right yesterday, didn't she? Looked rather well, I thought."

"Yes, she did," said Richard, but he felt a sick, guilty pang. He had taken her calm acceptance of the double life, with its deceptions, for granted; had it, in fact, been too much of a strain for her? There had been no signs of that at the weekend; she had shown her usual frank delight while they were together. He, of all people, knew there was much more to Kate than most people realized; but, like everyone else, she must have a breaking point.

"The police are on their way," said Dr. Wetherbee.

"Oh!" That disconcerted Richard, whose immediate instinct was to delay and wait for some sign from Kate if she had fled. "Is that wise?" he asked. "If she's just gone off, won't she either come back or telephone to say where she is?"

"Kate wouldn't lose her head just because the old lady went too far," said Dr. Wetherbee. "She might walk out in a fury but she'd soon come back, and she'd never let us down; she's far too conscientious. She'd telephone, at least. She may have gone for a drive last night and had an accident, though that doesn't account for the state of the kitchen. I think there's more to it. Anyway, I'll

112

come back as soon as I can, but it may be some time. You and Paul had better do what you can about my appointments. And maybe Marjorie Dodds can come in." He decided not to mention the severed airer on the telephone.

"All right. Don't worry—we'll cope," said Richard.

Dr. Wetherbee rang off and Richard sat for a moment staring at the telephone after he had replaced the receiver.

"Bad news, Doctor?" inquired the patient, briefly forgetting his own troubles in his interest in those of the doctor.

"Something unexpected's cropped up," said Richard. "Excuse me a minute."

He left his office and found Nurse Meadows scurrying past. Briefly he explained what had happened and asked her to ring up Marjorie Dodds or the other part-time helper, Mrs. Ford.

"Tell them to keep quiet about what's happened," Richard added. "We don't want to start a panic. There's probably a simple explanation and Kate will walk in at any minute."

He returned to his ulcer patient wondering what could have possessed Kate to have gone driving wildly round at night. She must have had an accident. Had she learned about the party last night and been hurt by her exclusion from it. He had suggested inviting her, but when Cynthia disagreed he had not pressed it; it was not worth making into an issue.

He had glanced, that morning, at the political news in the paper. Cynthia, whose day it was to help at the Senior Citizens' Club, had not looked at it at all.

The police, when they arrived at No. 11 in the shape of one constable, had at first taken the view that Kate, a woman on the verge of middle age and confined at home with an elderly mother, might have become hysterical and run away, but Dr.

Wetherbee's insistence, supported by Mrs. Burke, that it was highly improbable at last persuaded the constable to consider other possibilities.

"The wireless," Mrs. Burke said. "It was playing. Kate would never have left it on, wasting the battery. They cost money. And why would she cut down the airer? Tell me that. Wanton destruction, that is. And where's the rope gone? We'll want to put it up again."

Stepping out to inspect the garage, whence Kate's car had disappeared, the constable looked around. He was fifty years old, very experienced though slow to accept a new idea. However, he missed very little, and now he did not miss the footprints Gary had left on the soft ground outside the kitchen as he watched Kate through the window. He looked about and found more, leading to the back door. There were other marks, too, on the path and near the garage.

"Was the back door locked?" he asked Dr. Wetherbee, who did not know. But Mrs. Burke said that when she had gone to see if Kate's car was in the garage, the back door was unlocked.

The policeman looked at the marks on the ground, long scrape marks consistent with something being dragged along— something heavy, needing effort. He did not mention them, but instructed Mrs. Burke and Dr. Wetherbee not to walk over that area themselves.

Then he went to his car and rang in for help.

13

Gary had not wanted to let Kate out of his sight. He dragged her out to the garage and left her lying on the ground under a large bush while he opened the doors, which Kate never bothered to lock. After he released her legs from those of the chair, he bound them together before freeing the rest of her and retying her into a mummylike bundle. She had struggled so fiercely when he first surprised her that he would not risk trying to make her walk, even at the point of a knife. There was no problem about finding her car keys; he had noticed them on the dresser when he was preparing his meal.

Kate made herself sag as heavily as she could, so that his task was as difficult as possible, and as he dragged her along she uttered grunting protests which seemed very loud to Gary, but which in fact, because of the gag in her mouth, were no more than faint moans. Kate's Mini took up very little space in the large garage, so he had room to haul her alongside the car, open the door, and tip the bucket seat before heaving her into the back. A primitive instinct for self-preservation made Kate move her head to protect it, and bend her legs. Gary crammed her into the narrow space on the floor behind the two front seats. He pulled out her old raincoat and covered her with it; she could neither see nor be seen.

He started the car and reversed out of the garage, then got out and closed the doors. As an afterthought, he went back to the kitchen for the knife and pulled the raincoat back from her face to show it to her, touching her cheek with the blade, then covering her again. After that he drove into the road. He went past the turning where he had left his own car. It should be safe there until he could get back for it.

Suddenly, sickeningly, Gary realized that he had left his gloves in the Vauxhall; all this time he had been leaving fingerprints wherever he went.

He jammed on the brakes and stopped the car, crouching over the wheel and uttering a groan. Kate, beneath her cover, wondered what had happened as she was pitched forward and then back. She made some groaning sounds herself. Gary began to curse, sitting there. Should he go back? He would have to clean the whole kitchen, wash every plate and utensil he had used. There was the cupboard where he had hidden, the room where he had struggled with his prisoner. The task was too daunting: he would overlook something and lose valuable time. It was better to concentrate on getting rid of Mrs. Havant; he had left no clues in Wattleton, so there would be no reason for the police to link the two events.

While eating his bacon and eggs, Gary had thought of sending Mrs. Havant, in her car, over Beachy Head. If the car could be destroyed by fire, so much the better; then there would be no evidence that he had driven it, and his fingerprints in the woman's house did not prove violence. There had been no blood. As

116

he drove toward the center of Ferringham, looking for signposts to send him to the south, Gary tried to think of a way in which to manage what must look like an accident.

Kate, agonizingly uncomfortable on the floor of the car with her hands still behind her back and her legs trussed together, tried to move as soon as the car settled down to a steady motion. Her captor had stopped cursing now, and the subsequent near silence was eerie. She could hear the swish of the tires and the hum of the engine, but she had no impression of what speed they were traveling at, or of their direction. She could wriggle her toes and her fingers, and she could turn her head, but she was so tall that to straighten her back in the available space, or in any way relieve the drag on her arms, was impossible.

She tried to think constructively.

She was alive, and she had not, so far, been raped, both major items on the credit list. She had been so angry and frightened while this wild man, whose name she did not know, was cooking and eating his meal that she had not thought at all about him, but now she realized that though he was apparently starving, he was terrified, too; his bout of swearing since they drove away had betrayed panic as well as rage. She tried to breathe deeply and steadily; she would not show her fear, whatever happened.

She wouldn't be missed until the morning. Thank goodness it was one of Mrs. Burke's days, although her mother would start ringing her bell the moment she realized that Kate was late with her breakfast. She would ring and ring, Kate knew. In the end she might get up to see what had caused the delay. The effect of the Mogadon would have worn off; there was no chance that the old lady would oversleep. The police might be asked to look for Kate eventually, but no attempt to find her could begin for hours. She had no idea how much time had passed since she listened to the midnight news bulletin on the radio. The car stopped, then

117

jerked into bottom gear and went off again; traffic lights, she supposed. She could see nothing, and the taste of that soiled handkerchief in her mouth was vile.

She tried moving her head more vigorously; she might dislodge the raincoat from her face and be able to see streetlights, if there were any around, or at least remove the suffocating feeling that it gave her. After a few wriggles, she succeeded; she was glad of the raincoat over her body, for she would otherwise have been cold in her courtelle sweater and jersey skirt.

Gary drove on in silence, following the signs for Oxford. There would probably be a map in the car and he would stop in a quiet spot to look at it. He might have to get petrol, too. With the woman in the back, it would be risky, but he would find an unmanned self-service station. These Minis did a good mileage, he knew, but their tanks were small. He looked at the gauge. It was half full.

Kate had thought of this, too. She knew there were two or three gallons in the car; he would not have to stop yet.

After they had been driving for some time, Gary turned off the main road into a deserted lane that ran through a wooded area. He got out of the car to relieve himself; Kate could hear what was happening, as he had not moved away.

She would like to do the same thing, she realized, but how could she tell him so? Anyway, he'd never untie her and allow her out of the car. She'd have to hang on. It would be too humiliating if she lost control. That tea, drunk so long ago, was the regrettable cause of her present discomfort, one that was a minor matter compared with the peril she was in. Perhaps they'd reached the spot where he meant to rape and kill her; he'd have to untie her legs at least, and she might have a chance to fight

118

him. A kick could be enough. She looked up at the night sky, screened by trees. There were no stars.

Gary's bulk obscured the window. He opened the car door, peered into the back, and discovered her face exposed. Her eyes, above the gag, seen in the car's interior light, looked unafraid, not at all like Sandra King's eyes as she had fought beneath him.

"Look—Mrs. Havant—I'm sorry and all that. I didn't mean it, with that girl. It was the screaming, see? I had to shut her up. But you could tell them it was me. That's why I had to get you. It won't hurt. I'll do it some nice way. You understand that, don't you?"

Kate stared at him steadily over the gag. She would not shake her head, or nod, or give any sign of having understood.

He got back into the car, closing the door so that they were now in darkness, and went on talking, sitting in the driver's seat, looking forward at the night.

"It was all her fault. She wanted it—then she didn't. They often do, you know. Selling door to door, that's my job. Lots of them want it. You'd be surprised. Course, it's not worth pushing if they don't, even if you fancy them. There's always someone else. But there comes a point. And I hadn't had any for a bit."

Silence.

"I'd had a few drinks, too," he said, all too sober now.

He sat there, reflecting, in the darkness. Then he decided to look for a map. Unable to find the switch that worked the car's interior light, he opened the door a little, so that it came on. Kate's Mini was one of the old ones with large pockets in both doors, and he had put the knife in the one on his side. Now, rummaging among the clutter in it, he realized that he would not be able to grab the knife quickly if he needed it, so he put it on the glove shelf. He found a box of tissues, somewhat battered, a tin of polish so old that it was solid, an aerosol de-icer, and

119

various other items. No map. He tried the other door, and found a very old one, much worn and torn, published before most of the motorways now in use were even planned.

Gary's torch was in his own car, with the gloves, and the dim light made it hard to consult the map. He couldn't even find Ferringham for some time. The silence all around was unnerving to him, and suddenly he leaned over, untied the tea towel still bound round Kate's face, and pulled the gag from her mouth. He tried to do it gently.

The relief was so great that tears came into Kate's eyes. She blinked rapidly; she must show no sign of weakness. She ran her tongue round her dry mouth and closed her aching jaw.

"I took the Oxford road," Gary said. "I'm not sure how far we've come."

Kate could feel his fear, as she had earlier, in the kitchen. Suddenly an owl hooted outside and he started. He had un-gagged her not for her sake but for his: to have some conversation. If she stayed silent, he might turn violent, sour. If she could make some sort of contact with him, though, she might save herself. Wasn't that what happened when people were taken hostage or kidnapped? They got involved with their captors. She must play this one back to him.

"What's the time?" she asked. Her voice came as a croak from her dry throat.

"Half past two," said Gary, consulting his expensive digital watch.

Kate had expected to hear it was much later, and felt despair.

"We're going to Beachy Head," he said.

Beachy Head! This was a reprieve, for Beachy Head was a long way from Ferringham and would take hours to reach by any route. Kate had never been there, and was unsure of its precise location on the Sussex coast.

120

Gary got out of the car again, and, without untying her, pulled her, with some effort but not unkindly, up into a sitting position on the rear seat. The he showed her the knife.

"If anyone comes—if a car passes and you make a single sound—you get this," he threatened.

"I understand," Kate said.

The owl hooted again, and a screech owl answered it with a piercing shriek. Gary jumped.

"Those are only owls," said Kate.

"We can't stay here. It's much too quiet," said Gary illogically.

"No one will find us here," said Kate. "There'll be nothing coming along till morning. Why don't you get some sleep?"

It was a feeble attempt at a delaying tactic, but all she could think of, and she did not know he had slept that afternoon in the comfort of The Black Swan.

"I want to get to Beachy Head before morning," Gary said.

He must mean to tip her over it. Suicide. He meant it to look like that.

"They'll catch you, you know," Kate said. "The police will. You left fingerprints at my house."

"I've got no record," Gary said. "They'll not know who it was. I didn't leave anything at that flat. The girl's. I wiped everything I'd touched."

Kate tried again.

"You said you didn't mean to kill her," she said. "If you give yourself up and say so, it would just be manslaughter, not murder."

She wasn't sure of that, in fact, but it sounded possible.

"No, no. It wouldn't be. I'd go down for life."

"Well, that'd only be ten years or so," Kate said dryly. "You'd get out after that. Maybe less. If you kill me, too, it will be much worse. And that will be really murder."

"But they won't know. I'll be back at work later in the day. No one will connect me with you or with that Sandra," Gary said. "No one's seen me. No one else."

"Suppose I promise to say nothing?" Kate said. "If you let me go, that is, I'll only say I saw you at the roadside. I won't mention this. I could be home again before I'm missed."

"I couldn't trust you," Gary said. "Sorry. It's nothing personal, Mrs. Havant."

The way he was speaking to her, almost with deference, calling her Mrs. Havant, gave Kate a surge of hope. She was silent, trying to think of arguments to put to him. Delay, delay, she thought; keep him talking; by ten o'clock at the latest, someone would surely start to search for her.

But they'd never look in Sussex, and by then, if his plans worked, it would be too late. And no one would connect her disappearance with the death of Sandra King.

Well, Richard would be safe, at least. He would never know why this had happened to her, so that he could in no way blame himself; he would be able to continue his marriage and his career free from threat. For if she was dead, there would be no new evidence for Cynthia and her private eye.

"How did you find me?" she asked.

"I went to that pub in Risely. The girl—Sandra"—he stumbled over the name—"she said you were going there. I went all the way to that place in the country first, that you'd given as your address. You gave a false one," he said accusingly.

So this was the man who had called on Betty, not a detective. In spite of her plight, Kate felt relief; Cynthia knew nothing yet.

"But how did you discover my real one?" she asked. "It was clever of you," she added cunningly.

"I went back to that pub—The Black Swan," said Gary. "They knew you were friendly with the doctor. I went to his place first. There was a party or something going on. I saw you in the road."

He had found her by chance. What if she hadn't gone out last night? He'd have found her address in the end, through Richard—followed him, maybe, in the morning, and seen her at the Health Centre. But if she'd stayed at home she might be safely asleep in her own bed now; and if she had done her duty as a citizen and reported seeing this man to the police, she might have avoided this present danger.

"I had to get you quick," Gary explained, almost apologizing. "You'd have rung the fuzz."

Would she, in the end?

They sat in silence, the night round them very still. Gary put his hand out to start the car, and Kate spoke.

"Before you go on, you've just relieved yourself. I need to, too," she said. "I promise not to try to escape, if you'll untie me long enough."

She knew now that he did not mean to rape her. Perhaps he found her unattractive—most men did, though she'd an idea rapists weren't too fussy. But if she could get him to grant this request, she—or, rather, Mrs. Havant—would have established a small victory over him. She would also be a lot more comfortable, and therefore braver. He might leave her mouth untied, and if so, she could talk to him, try to persuade him that it was hopeless to go on, and that the police would catch him in the end for Sandra's death, if not for hers. If he unbound her and tied her up again, she might, by clenching her muscles and holding her breath, find that when she relaxed there would be some slack in her bonds. If so, she might have a chance to free herself.

Gary thought for a few moments.

"You wouldn't get far if you did try running," he said at last. "I'd soon catch you."

Kate wasn't so sure. But he probably would, since her limbs were stiff and cramped from being bound so long.

He untied her, even handed her the box of tissues from the

car, and though he stayed near her as she stumbled over the grass, he turned his head away.

"Thank you. I'm ready now," she said eventually, in a firm voice. "Would you tie my arms in front? They were very painful the way you did them before. And I should like to put my rain-coat on. It's cold." She made these requests in an authoritative voice, as though refusal were inconceivable.

Gary opposed neither; moreover, he told her to sit in the front of the car, bundling her trussed form in beside him.

They drove on, stopping once for petrol at an all-night self-service station. Outside Oxford, Gary misread a sign at a round-about and they had traveled ten miles before he realized that he was getting no nearer to Newbury, the next town on his route to the south. Kate had seen his mistake and wondered how long it would be before he saw it himself. A few more such errors would use time precious to both of them, and dawn would be that much closer. He crouched at the wheel, peering anxiously ahead; it was not easy to pick up all the signs at junctions.

Gary cursed again, furiously, when he understood what he had done. He turned the car and drove back, much faster. After a while he slowed down to a steadier pace, and Kate wondered if he had thought that a speeding Mini, in the small hours, might attract notice if a police patrol car was around. If only one would come along! But it didn't. She remained silent through all this, the seat belt tight across her body, but as she sat there she worked her wrists and her ankles unobtrusively, trying to loosen their bonds.

The road to Newbury was good in places, but in others un-dulating and narrow. Gary roared along the dual carriageway sections, but when they came up behind a long lorry on an older stretch of road and had to stay behind it, Kate felt his tension increase. She blessed the delay as Gary sat on the lorry's tail waiting for a chance to pass. The small car's engine hummed steadily, the body emitting the various squeaks and rattles Kate knew were harmless, just symptoms of its age. If only it would break down, she thought. But it didn't.

Outside Newbury, Gary stopped and spent more time consulting the map. He seemed to be having problems with the pages where the sections joined, and for some time he gazed at the map of the south coast looking for Beachy Head. It was marked in tiny print; Kate could not see it herself, gazing down at the map which he had pulled across the hand brake between them so that he could benefit from the Mini's dim interior light. Eventually he took a ball-point pen from his pocket and circled it. It was a still a long way off, Kate saw thankfully.

"Basingstoke and Guildford," Gary muttered, starting the engine and putting the car into gear. Main routes were best.

Basingstoke wasn't far from Newbury; they seemed to get there very quickly, but instead of a town they met complex roundabout systems and direction indicators. Since Kate's map had been published, the area had become a vast industrial overspill, with housing projects on what was once agricultural land and suburbs where there had been villages. Guildford was signposted, but not on every board, and when in doubt Gary should have followed the motorway directions, but he knew he did not want to go to London, so at an early roundabout he took a different outlet. Soon they were heading toward Reading, and when Gary saw that once again he had turned the wrong way, he decided not to turn back but to cut south and pick up the road they should be on.

Now they were in a country lane. Trees bordered the narrow black ribbon of the road as it wound ahead in the lights of the car. Bright glints from the eyes of animals were reflected back, not man-made cat's eyes. Gary had to travel slowly or risk running into the ditch. They emerged, eventually, onto a main road. Kate was sure the way for Guildford lay to the left, but Gary turned right. It was almost funny when they reached the outskirts of Basingstoke again.

Gary stopped with a squealing of the Mini's brakes, so that Kate was brought sharply against the restraining strap of her seat belt. He sat there, cursing.

"You should have told me I was on the wrong road," he said at last.

"I'm not your map reader," Kate snapped back.

By now the sky was growing light. She stared out. Was it her imagination? No, there were streaks of pale gray appearing, so that must be the east. She hoped this realization would not occur to her captor. If he decided to steer by the rising sun, his navigation might improve.

He drove on again, and entered Basingstoke carefully, looking out for signs. Proceeding slowly, Gary found the place where they should have turned the first time, toward the motorway, but though they were soon on the proper road, Kate knew that he was now thoroughly disconcerted.

He drove on, once or twice stamping on the brake as an animal scurried across their path, or more bright eyes showed in the headlights.

"You're not used to the country, are you?" Kate asked at last.

"No. I don't like it," Gary said. "It's too quiet."

"Where's your home? Where were you born?"

"In Nottingham. I've not been back for years. Had lots of jobs," he said. "I'm working for a publisher at present."

"Do you enjoy it?" asked Kate.

"It's all right. I'm going in for property, though," said Gary.

"In what way?"

"Buying and selling. You get a house, see—then you do it up—turn it into flats—let them off. Buy another and do the same

126

again." Gary knew what Mrs. Fitzgibbon was paid by her various guests; the same house turned into bed-sitters and with no catering provided would bring in a much higher return. He explained all this to Kate, who said she found it interesting, which was true. No. 11 could be turned into flats, if there was the money to pay for the renovation, she had often thought. In other circumstances, she and Gary might have had a rewarding conversation.

"Don't try chatting me up," he said, suddenly angry. "I won't go soft on you."

Kate gripped her hands together. The cord round her wrists was definitely looser.

"I wasn't chatting you up," she said mildly. "I've often thought of doing up my house. It's rather big."

"It's not half old-fashioned," Gary said. "That old sink you've got."

Kate didn't reply, and after a while he spoke again.

"Sorry. I didn't mean to be rude, Mrs. Havant. I'm a bit on edge."

Soon after that he turned down a lane, to answer another call of nature, Kate supposed. He pulled the car into a gateway and departed into the now graying surroundings with a handful of tissues.

He certainly was edgy, and this time he might be gone for several minutes.

She tried to bend forward. Her wrists were slacker than before, and if she could bring them to reach her ankles she might be able to untie the knot around them; however, the old-fashioned seat belt held her too firmly, and if she undid it, she might not be able to refasten it, so that when he came back he would discover what she had been doing. She tried raising her legs, bringing her ankles up against her thighs with an enormous effort, and, panting as she twisted in her seat, felt for the knot. She pulled and

127

tugged at it, and managed to undo one hitch. Moving her legs, she felt the cord give slightly.

She dared not attempt more now, in case he caught her. She looked at the knife, lying there, out of reach, on the shelf.

When Gary came back, looking pale, he asked her if she wanted to get out.

She would have liked to, but if she did, he would discover she had undone her ankles, so she thanked him and refused.

"Next time you stop, please," she said.

"Next time's Beachy Head," said Gary.

14

The headquarters of World-Wide Encyclopaedias were in a small
office over a warehouse in Deptford. When their office was open
on Wednesday morning, they were soon able to name the representative covering the Wattleton area. Gary Browne lived at the
Grange Residential Hotel, and they expected to hear from him
that day. Representatives had a lot of freedom, but they telephoned progress and mailed their reports regularly. The firm did
not provide them with cars, and the managing director did not
know what make Gary's was; Gary merely claimed a mileage
allowance.

"What's all this about?" he asked the sergeant who interviewed
him, a member of the Metropolitan Police called in to help his
provincial colleagues.

But the Sergeant would not tell him.

Mrs. Fitzgibbon at the Grange Residential Hotel was not
pleased when two policemen called there later that morning. It
did the hotel no good to see their car outside, or them on her

step. She admitted them to the residents' lounge, anxious to get whatever it was over quickly. Maybe the new Spanish cook's papers weren't in order.

An aroma of fried bacon still clung about the hall, and the lounge smelled of stale tobacco when the two men from the Wattleton force entered. Mrs. Fitzgibbon was surprised when they asked about Gary Browne.

Yes, he had been staying there for three months and was a model guest. He kept his room neat and was quiet. He was often away, but retained the room on a weekly basis, paying in advance; this was quite usual: a lot of her gentlemen traveled but they wanted a base. Mr. Browne hadn't been in last night, but he was there for breakfast yesterday and on Monday morning.

Nothing had happened to him, had it?

They were merely checking. Routine, said the sergeant. Might they see his room?

Mrs. Fitzgibbon had nothing to conceal, and she hoped none of her gentlemen had either, least of all that nice young Mr. Browne. She showed them into Gary's room.

It was very tidy. His brush and comb were on the light oak chest, and a cheap alarm clock stood on the bedside table. The policeman put these items into polythene bags, carefully labeling and sealing them. All should show prints, and there were several nice long hairs clinging to the brush, though it was clean. Finally the sergeant looked in the wardrobe. Right at the back, tucked away, bundled on the floor, was the brown suit Gary had worn for his journey to Kent. It was torn and muddied from his passage over gardens and fences and eventually through Mrs. McBride's shopwindow. There was a pair of shoes, also muddy, on the wardrobe floor.

Mrs. Fitzgibbon, baffled by all this, made no objection when the policemen packed everything up and gave her a receipt.

130

They asked if she knew the number of Gary Browne's car and she looked it up for them. She kept a record of all her gentlemen's cars. It was white, she said; she wasn't sure of the make, but the odd-job man would know. He was out at the back just now, mending a gutter.

It was a Ford Escort, the odd-job man confirmed.

"But he'd got a new one Monday. A Vauxhall," he reported. "Yellow. Didn't see the number."

He seemed quite certain.

Richard's morning had been hectic, dealing with Dr. Wetherbee's patients as well as his own, and it was half past one before he went home to lunch. He sat at the dining-room table facing the plate of chicken and salad which Cynthia had left ready for him under a silver cover before she went off to her Senior Citizens.

Whatever could have come over Kate?

Women hitherto calm and controlled could sometimes act unreasonably. They got depressed. Even Cynthia, usually equable, had been known to have moods, though most of her worries were of a trivial domestic nature. But for Kate to vanish—that was incomprehensible. He pushed a piece of chicken round his plate and studied it in perplexity. Could she have become hysterical?

Richard put the morsel of chicken into his mouth and chewed it slowly. Eventually, he swallowed it. Then he gave up. He'd flush the rest of the meal down the lavatory, so that Cynthia wouldn't discover he hadn't eaten it.

Before he could do so, the front-door bell rang.

Dr. Wetherbee stood outside, his Rover parked on the gravel beside the bed of Moon Maiden roses, always such a show in summer.

"What's the news? Has she been found? Did she smash up her car?" Richard hurled the questions at him. Dr. Wetherbee had not returned to the Health Centre all morning.

"No, she hasn't been found," said Dr. Wetherbee, whose face was grim; he looked suddenly old. "It's unbelievable," he went on. "The police think someone's—well—kidnapped Kate. Abducted her. There's been no accident notified involving her car. That old airer thing in the kitchen, you remember—you must have seen it—it's been cut down and the rope that strung it up has gone. Sort of clothesline stuff—cord, you know. Not plastic. I got the impression they think she was tied up with it. There were some footprints in the garden by the kitchen window and the back door, and rub marks, funny sort of smears, as if some heavy bundle had been dragged along the ground. They think someone may have broken in—a thief—and Kate surprised him, so he tied her up. At some point he cooked a meal. It can't have been Kate who made all that mess—there was a tea tray of hers in the sitting room, and whoever ate in the kitchen took sugar in their tea. Kate doesn't."

No, she didn't. Richard knew it, too.

"As far as one can tell, nothing's been stolen. But a particularly sharp knife is missing from the kitchen, Mrs. Burke says."

"My God!"

"It must have happened last night, so goodness knows how long she's been gone," Dr. Wetherbee continued. "Kate's bed was turned down, with a hot-water bottle in it and her nightdress on the top. Poor Kate. It was cold last night. I suppose she liked to hug the bottle. Better than nothing."

"What are the police doing?" Richard asked. "I mean, how are they trying to find her?" He spoke very carefully, trying to sound calm.

"They're looking for her car. It's gone, after all. And we know the number. Mrs. Burke knew it. I couldn't remember it."

Richard repeated the number immediately.

"Yes, that's right," Dr. Wetherbee said. "I shan't forget it again, I've heard it so often this morning."

"How did they—whoever it was—get into the house?" Richard asked.

"There's no sign of a forced entry. Kate always put the chain up on the front door last thing, and she hadn't done that or Mrs. Burke wouldn't have been able to get in this morning. She has a front-door key. The back door was unlocked and the key was on the kitchen dresser."

"So he could have just walked in."

"It seems like that."

"Silly girl. Fancy not locking the door," said Richard. Cynthia was a great one for barricading herself in the house after dark, with every bolt rammed home.

"I expect she's done it a thousand times—sat there with the door unlocked," said Dr. Wetherbee. "It's a quiet area, after all. You know, I can't help wondering if there could be any connection with that other business—that girl who was murdered in Wattleton last weekend. Raped and suffocated, she was. Or suffocated first. There was no robbery then, just things thrown around to make it look like one." Dr. Wetherbee's wife had followed every detail of the case and made sure he did, too. "Whoever did that got into the place easily—was let in by the girl herself, it's implied."

"But Wattleton's miles from here," said Richard.

"Yes. And that girl was much younger than Kate. She was found in her own flat, too. She didn't disappear." In fact, the fanciful theory he was expounding wasn't Dr. Wetherbee's own, but his wife's, made when he telephoned to warn that he would be late for lunch and giving the reason. It seemed even more unlikely when he mentioned it himself. "The police want to find a man with a white car who helped that other girl change a wheel

133

on Friday evening, somewhere south of Risely. I suppose you didn't see this fellow, Richard? You went to Birmingham on Friday. You must have come back that way."

"I didn't come home that night," said Richard. "I spent the night at The Black Swan at Risely."

"Did you? Oh, well, you couldn't have seen him, then."

"What exactly do the police want to know?" Richard asked.

Dr. Wetherbee told him.

Richard had not seen the man who stopped to help Sandra King, but Kate might have done so; she hadn't mentioned it, but she had been on that road at the time in question.

The police had now established the identity of the man who had helped Sandra King change the wheel of her car. Fingerprints on Gary Browne's hairbrush, on the encyclopedia bought by Madge Billings, on the boot jack and wheel brace in Sandra's car, and less distinctly on the rim of the damaged wheel all tallied. The clothes found in his wardrobe and the hair strands on the brush were being examined in the lab, and meanwhile a general call had gone out for him. The mud on his suit and shoes and the torn state of the garments were confusing.

"That young constable—Berry—he seems an alert fellow," said Detective Chief Superintendent Hawksworth.

"We'd have soon got round to encyclopedia salesmen without him, sir," said Bailey. "The first bookseller we saw this morning mentioned them at once."

"The lad used his wits," said Hawksworth.

Berry had merely done his duty, Bailey thought; he did not say so, however. Hawksworth was sometimes known as Hawk the Heart among officers with tougher attitudes, but he was ruthless in pursuit of real villains.

"Pity about the car," said Bailey. The computer still declared Gary Browne to be the owner of the Ford Escort whose number Mrs. Fitzgibbon had supplied; if he had sold it, the information had not yet been recorded. However, its number had been circulated and patrols all over the country would be watching for it; dealers would be asked about it, too.

"Points to his guilt over the girl," said Hawksworth. "Why turn it in, otherwise?"

"Cool customer, out selling his books on Monday as if nothing was wrong," said Bailey.

"Yes." Hawksworth was thoughtful, tapping his pen on the clean sheet of blotting paper in front of him. "That lad Berry—his remark about the break-in down in Kent. The report in the paper."

"Oh, yes, sir," said Bailey, without enthusiasm.

"It might explain the mud," said Hawksworth. "And the woman—what was her name, the shopkeeper?—she had, as Berry pointed out, spent the weekend in Risely."

"Yes, sir."

"I think we'd better get on to them down there—Fotherhurst, wasn't it? We've got Browne's shoes, after all, and a lot of mud, according to the report."

"Soil, sir. Earth," Bailey said.

"Earth, then. Tell them, Bailey. Might clear up their problem for them, if it is the same man."

"Shall we send a shoe and some soil down?" asked Bailey.

"No," Hawksworth replied. "Let them come to us."

15

Richard did not waste another second. He rushed from the house, leaving Dr. Wetherbee staring after him in amazement. If Kate, going to Risely, had seen the man with the white car, that man might have seen her and would know she could identify him. If he was the girl's killer, was it conceivable that he might somehow have got hold of Kate and abducted her? It seemed a wild, remote chance that he would find her, since she was staying at the hotel under an assumed name and had not given her address; he would have to trace her not only to the hotel but from there to Ferringham. If he had somehow managed the first, he might have followed her home, then waited for a chance to find her alone. The whole idea seemed incredible, but then so was Kate's disappearance.

Richard drove straight to Ferringham police station. The sergeant at the desk knew him, and admitted him immediately to Chief Inspector Meredith's office without requiring more explanation than that it was an urgent matter connected with Miss

Kate Wilson's disappearance. That disappearance was giving the station some exercise outside its usual experience, for abductions were infrequent in the area.

Richard told Meredith the facts crisply. He and Kate had met at the hotel in Risely on Friday evening. She had not mentioned seeing a girl with a puncture or a man with a white car, but she could have done so.

"In that case, wouldn't she have come forward, Dr. Stearne, and told us?"

"She might not have known about the police appeal," said Richard. "I'd not really taken it in myself, until someone else mentioned it." Then he added, "But she might not have wanted to involve me."

He did not need to explain. Meredith was too experienced to show surprise at anything, and he agreed that Kate's disappearance must be reported straight away to the C.I.D. at Wattleton. On the whole, however, he thought the two cases most unlikely to be linked.

Richard went back to the Health Centre where he had a surgery at half past two for which he was already late. He could do no more to help Kate. Meredith had confirmed what Dr. Wetherbee had already told him: there were marks consistent with the dragging of a body—"Not necessarily dead," Meredith had hastened to point out—on the path to Kate's garage. There were fingerprints all over the kitchen—on the cooker, the pans—in the hall, and in Kate's sitting room, all alien to the three sets predominating in the house, those of Kate, her mother, and Mrs. Burke.

"But it isn't fingerprints you want now, Inspector. It's Kate," Richard had said, though he could see that in fact the police were treating the case as one of extreme urgency already.

"Yes, Dr. Stearne, but if the prints were those of a known

villain, we'd know who to look for," the inspector explained. "We're looking for her car. When we find that—well—" He left the sentence unfinished.

Kate had been gone for hours; it must have been midnight, or even earlier, when the horror began. Richard, peering down a child's infected throat, had a vision of Kate with her throat cut.

That other girl's throat hadn't, in fact, been cut; but who would ever know what terrors she had faced before the ultimate one of death? If it was the same man who had abducted Kate, Richard was to blame. He had led her into their affair for no stronger reason in the beginning than that he was intrigued. Her shy response, and the ardor that developed with experience, still charmed him. He longed for their meetings but was glad to be spared anything more complicated, more demanding. She had yielded to him easily after the surprise they shared, that first time now so long ago. Had he not behaved, in fact, no better than the man who had raped Sandra King? The difference was that Sandra had resisted. It did not make Richard's guilt the less: he was no better than a common rapist. Kate had not been the slightest bit in love with him; she had still hankered, at that time, for Paul Fox, though Richard believed she got over that when she had a real affair to think about. They had become affectionate friends; perhaps that was the perfect foundation for a relationship, not the fireworks of intense physical attraction and very little else, so that the rest had to be won, often painfully over years, and sometimes never was.

Cynthia would have to know. Whatever had happened to Kate—even if after all, her disappearance was unrelated to the murder of Sandra King—he would not hope to spare Cynthia from learning the truth now, and he could not expose her to the humiliation of learning it from the police or some other source.

138

She might walk out. She might report him to the B.M.A. None of that mattered, beside the danger to Kate.

At Wattleton, P. C. Berry's wife and her friend Madge Billings had helped to build photofit pictures of the encyclopedia salesman who had called on them. Mrs. Fitzgibbon of the Grange Residential Hotel had built up a likeness of her lodger Gary Browne. All tallied remarkably, and were circulated to the police throughout the country, to the press, and to television. Meanwhile, the police were trying to trace Gary Browne's family to get a real photograph of him. Mrs. Fitzgibbon had been able to describe the clothes he was probably wearing: the tan safari jacket and darker slacks which he had on on Tuesday morning.

The call from Chief Inspector Meredith at Ferringham surprised Bailey, but he listened carefully to the account of Kate Wilson's disappearance. Here was the Risely connection again; it must be taken seriously. Meredith agreed to send a messenger up at once with samples of the fingerprints found in the house in Chestnut Avenue. They would soon prove whether or not Gary Browne and the abductor of Miss Wilson were the same man.

It seemed a long shot, but it was a possibility; and if he was the same man, Bailey didn't give much for the chances of the missing woman.

Halfway through the afternoon, between patients, Paul came into Richard's office.

"I've got a lull," he remarked, heedless of the fact that Richard had not. "I say, what's all this to-do about Kate? I went past the house this morning and there were police everywhere. She

139

hasn't really been kidnapped, has she? Someone'd have got a ransom call by now. Why Kate, for God's sake? Surely it's more likely that the worm's turned at last and she blipped the old lady on the head and fled?"

Richard, seated at his desk, looked up at the bulky, red-faced man with dislike.

"The police are sure she's been kidnapped—abducted—call it what you like," he said stiffly. "There's a chance it may be connected with the murder of that girl in Wattleton at the weekend."

"No! You mean the one there's all this fuss about in the papers?" Paul exclaimed. "But that's a sex case—she was raped, wasn't she? Surely that can't have happened to our Kate? Who would want to do her? She's no luscious chick."

"Any woman, old or young, can be raped, as you should know," Richard said austerely. "It happens all the time—even within marriage." Paul must hear the same sad tales as he did, from his female patients.

"Well, reading between the lines, this girl led him on and then said no," said Paul.

"You don't know that. No one knows what happened, except the two concerned. Why shouldn't she say no?"

His hands were shaking, and Paul noticed it.

"I say, you're in a state," he said, and added, amazed, "About Kate?"

"Aren't you? Don't you give a damn about what may be happening to her at this very moment?" demanded Richard. "She may be dead—horribly dead—for all we know."

"Well, of course I care—poor old Kate. But not to get the shakes about it," Paul said. "She's been around a long time and we'll miss her. It'll be terrible if she's suffered, but you must admit she's no ball of fire. Just a dull, efficient middle-aged girl. She'd never be anything else—an elderly girl eventually, of

140

course, if she comes back safe and sound, as I hope she will."

"The middle-aged girl, as you call her"—even as he spoke, Richard saw how Kate could seem just that to so many—"has the ability to be a warm and loving woman, like most normal females. She's been stifled by that bitch of a mother and she's been too dutiful to park her in a home and make a life of her own. Maybe too much lacking in confidence, after years of nagging and carping. We're to blame, too. We've made use of her here—we've been thankful to have someone so good—so capable and quiet that you scarcely notice her around and yet when she isn't here, it's chaos. Look what today's been like. She copes with all emergencies—she keeps our records straight and deals with all our bloody forms—she puts flowers in the waiting room." He almost said, And she wasted her best years imagining herself to be in love with you; but he held that bit back, glowering at Paul.

"Good heavens, there's no need to get in such a state—you'll send your blood pressure up, Dick," said Paul. "I didn't know you cared. Does she?"

Richard made an effort to speak more calmly.

"I'm sorry—I don't suppose you meant it, Paul, but you sounded very callous," he said.

"I'm sure I didn't intend to. Of course I hope poor old Kate isn't in the clutches of some sex fiend. But maybe he's a gentle rapist. That might do her good. She must be quite untouched. No one could get near her with that mother, even if they wanted to."

Richard's wrath surged again.

"It may interest you to know," he said, getting to his feet and glaring at Paul, his own face almost as red with rage as Paul's was from good living and his recent trip to Tenerife, "that Kate has been my mistress for the last five years. She's very dear to me."

He sat down abruptly after saying that. Kate might be dead,

141

but this unperceptive man who called himself a doctor must understand she had been desired; even, Richard admitted to himself, loved.

"Oh, my God!" said Paul.

"That may be the reason for what has happened," Richard said more quietly. "She may have seen this man they're looking for—the one who helped that girl change a wheel—when she was on the way to meet me. We stayed at Risely last weekend. He may have got her."

"God!" Paul wanted to ask a dozen questions but sheer stupefaction stopped him. "Well, maybe it needn't come out," he said, taking up what was, to him, the most important point. "I won't tell anyone—about you and her, I mean. You'll be all right, old man." Poor Richard; imagine wanting to have it off with Kate! Of course, he had few opportunities to escape from Cynthia, was bald and middle-aged, and it couldn't be easy for him if he wanted a bit on the side, as anyone might after a while. "Cynthia doesn't know, does she?"

"Not yet," said Richard heavily. "I'm going to tell her when I get home."

"Don't be such a fool. Now, listen to me," said Paul. "You don't want the sort of trouble that will give you. Cynthia wouldn't like it a bit, especially its being Kate—so different from her," he added hastily, lest Richard understood that he really meant Cynthia would be insulted if she learned that Richard's adulterous partner was just poor old Kate. "Surely your part in it all needn't come out? The police will be discreet—say she was meeting a Mr X. Meredith's a sensible chap."

"That's all you can think about, is it? Getting me off the hook?"

"And Cynthia. Why punish her and Philip for what you've done?" said Paul. "Think of the scandal."

"I can only think of Kate," said Richard.

142

"I can see that," said Paul dryly. "But keep your head. A reprimand from the B.M.A. won't help Kate, especially if she's dead, and it will do a lot of harm to Cynthia and Philip. There'd be nastly talk round Ferringham."

Richard's sudden rage had burnt itself out. There was truth in Paul's remarks.

"I'll think about it," he said. "Perhaps I need say nothing yet."

"Let me know if I can help," Paul said. "Sorry, and all that."

He went away, amazed.

"Whoever would have thought it," he murmured to himself when he was back in his own office. "Richard and poor old Kate! Well!"

16

Kate thought, I must be able to do something.

She tried to move her legs. Though she had undone one hitch of the knot that tied them, they were still securely fastened, but if she persevered, the next loop might work loose. It would be a slow business, though, and her hands were still bound.

"They'll start looking for me early, you know," she said. "I'll be missed quite soon."

"You won't. You're a widow. You live alone," said Gary.

"I live with my mother. She was in bed when you broke in last night," said Kate. "The police will look for my car."

"We'll be in Sussex by then," said Gary. "We'll have reached Beachy Head. It'll be over." He meant she'd be dead, but he could not tell her so, bluntly.

"Well, they'll catch you," Kate said. "No one will believe I drove myself over the cliff, if that's what you're planning. Or jumped. Especially tied up like this. The police aren't stupid.

They'll know that whoever did it was the same person who killed that girl."

"I didn't kill her. It was an accident, I told you," said Gary. "And they'll never know it was me."

"They'll find you. Other people must have seen you besides me. You can't kill them all. And what about your job? Won't they wonder where you are?"

"As long as I send in my returns, it's OK," said Gary. "I'm my own boss."

He'd ring in, once the job was done; they'd expect a call this morning. They'd have no reason to suspect he wasn't speaking from Wattleton. And he'd go back to the Grange Residential Hotel, chat up Mrs. Fitzgibbon, resume his routine. Even though his prints were all over Mrs. Havant's house, there was no way the police could find out whose they were; the only lead to him was his car, parked in that road nearby, and he must collect it quickly. It had brochures and encyclopedia samples in the back, and it could be traced to him. But he couldn't go back in Mrs. Havant's Mini, for, as she had said, the police would be searching for it when she was missed, and anyway he meant to ditch her in it.

Perhaps he should get rid of her now. Was there time to get back with her car before her disappearance was discovered? All that about her mother might be true; she didn't seem like someone who told lies; she was a nice sort of person.

Gary drove on more slowly. Perhaps Beachy Head wasn't such a good idea, but how could he stage some other accident? He'd have to knock her on the head in any case, first, before he sent her over, and he didn't want to do that; he didn't like violence.

He turned left at the next crossroads and began to drive north. He wouldn't go back the way they had come; with the day begin-

145

ning, the main roads would be dangerous if the police were looking for her. He'd deal with her some other way.

Kate said nothing when he changed direction. He could not really have repented and be taking her home unharmed.

"This geezer—this doctor chap—why didn't you marry him?" Gary suddenly asked.

"He's married already," said Kate. If this man killed her, and the police caught him, the truth about her meetings with Richard was bound to come out. "And I have to look after my mother," she added stiffly.

"Ill, is she?"

"Delicate," Kate said.

"Lucky for her—your mother, I mean—that your husband died, then. What happened to him?"

"He didn't die. I never said I was a widow," Kate replied. "You assumed it."

"So you're not. Walked out on you, did he? Bet it was because of the old lady—your mum. Doesn't do, living all on top of each other. Though you've a big house. Been there long?"

"Quite a time," said Kate.

"I've changed my mind about Beachy Head," Gary told her. "It's too far. I've got another plan."

He hadn't yet, but he hoped one would come to him. He couldn't gas her with exhaust fumes, which would be a peaceful way to die, as he had no hose to connect to the car. It was a pity about that. He could have unbound her afterward. He didn't want to wait till the shops were open and he could buy one.

Now he was back in alien territory with hedgerows on either side of the road, patches of wood, meadows. It was getting much lighter; the moon floated out from behind a cloud, pale in the early morning sky. People would soon be about.

Kate went on moving her wrists and trying to free her legs. She

146

was not having much success. She thought of undoing the seat belt when all her captor's attention was on the road, and then lunging against him so that he piled up the car. It would be a better end than being killed by him, and it might finish him off as well as herself. On the other hand, neither of them might be hurt and he would be very angry. It wasn't a very good idea, but she decided to concentrate on it; an appropriate moment to try it might come.

They passed through several villages, curtains still drawn in the houses now visible in the gray dawn; no one looking from a window in this peaceful region and seeing the Mini pass would believe it was being driven by a murderer.

Gary saw the lane suddenly, and braked hard. It was a narrow, rutted track, leading off to the left, apparently going nowhere. He switched off the car lights and turned up it, the Mini bumping over the rough ground. The lane might lead to a farm, but as they slowly continued, in low gear, no house came into view. Kate thought of Chodbury St. Mary, where at this hour milk lorries might be coming down such tracks, or tractors pulling trailers bearing churns to leave at the road's end for collection. She sat alert, hoping to meet a tractor head-on, or at least to reach a farmhouse with a dog that would bark loudly and warn of strangers. But they met nothing and they saw no building.

The lane led on, uphill and past trees. They had traveled along it for more than a mile between well-trimmed hedges showing the faintest tinge of green. Then came a stretch of blackthorn, the blossom white, and Kate shivered; there was always a cold spell, the blackthorn winter, even after days of warm weather, when that came out.

They reached the quarry suddenly. The track widened; there were wire fences on either side and beyond them, and a warning notice:"DISUSED QUARRY. DANGER. KEEP OUT."

147

Gary got out of the car, climbed over the fence, and went to the quarry's edge. It was quite light enough now to see the steep drop at that side, though the track, which once lorries must have used, continued downward. The stone was white; it was a chalk quarry.

He came back to the car, smiling.

"This will do very nicely," he said.

Kate said, "You'll have a very long walk if you tip me over the top of there in the car."

Gary knew this was true; and he'd have to pass those thick hedges full of wild creatures, the fields of cattle that might escape, and, above all, he would be surrounded by the weird country quiet, which gave him the creeps.

And he had to get back to Ferringham fast, to collect his car.

He could throw her over the side just as she was, bound up, and go down afterward to untie her and make it look more like suicide. Her body might not be found for ages; there'd be no reason for anyone to look for her here, so far from where she lived. He could drive off then, in her car, to some point where he'd be able to catch a train or a bus, and abandon the Mini.

But it must be covered with his fingerprints, and they'd match those in the house. He'd never manage to clean them off the car. So it wouldn't be any use trying to fake a suicide, and he'd never get her to write a note, even if he had any paper; the threat of the knife, when she was under sentence of death anyway, would not be enough. He understood that much about her.

Gary went to the edge of the quarry and looked over. There might be a hut or a cave down there, a place where he could dump her. Shrubs and trees grew from the steep sides where the soil had not been disturbed for years; he couldn't see the whole area at the bottom. He'd have to take a look.

148

Gary did not think of walking around the perimeter. He returned to the car, started it again, and drove forward through the gap in the wire and up the slight slope that led to the mouth of the track winding down the quarry. Slowly, in low gear, the Mini crept down.

At the foot of the track there was a level area, and two sheds, one large and one much smaller. Both were dilapidated: their doors hung open, their sides were broken, and their roofs had fallen in; rafters pointed to the sky, with here and there a few tiles remaining. Gary stopped the car, got out, and went to look at them. If he left her here, in one of these sheds, bound and gagged, he need not actually kill her; she'd just die. It would be much easier like that. He'd have to keep her car, though, till he was well clear of the area. Then it would be best to burn it. That would destroy all evidence that he'd been in it.

Kate, watching him moving around, wondered what he was thinking. He was not insane; he knew very well what he was doing, and he did not want to commit another violent act. It was fear that had made him kill Sandra King; it was fear that had made him twist Kate's arms and threaten her with the knife; fear would compel him to kill her if he could.

The knife lay there, on the glove shelf, to the right of the steering wheel and below it. Kate could move her feet, though they were still tied together, and she had a little movement in her wrists and fingers—very little. If she could wriggle across into the driver's seat, she might be able to reach forward and grasp the knife.

She watched him. He had walked some distance from the car now, and was staring at the larger shed, a long low building with a gaping hole in one wall. Kate pressed her hands against her body; thank goodness her car had the sort of seat belt that fastened in front of the wearer, not on the floor; she'd never have reached round to undo one of those, but she managed this one.

She could move across the car easily now. Was it better to free her legs properly or make a quick bid for the knife? Without it, she couldn't undo herself enough to run.

It was the knife she needed. She raised her hips, pressing against the floor of the car with her feet, and wriggled her buttocks across the space between the two bucket seats, over the hand brake and the gear lever. It wasn't difficult to pull her legs across afterward; the whole operation took seconds but it seemed like hours.

She reached beyond the steering wheel, groping with her hands. She must be certain that she held the knife securely before she lifted it out; it would be so easy to drop it. She caught it between her fingers and drew back; the knife did fall, but by then it was over her knees and lay on her lap. She tried turning her wrists against it there, but could get no purchase on it, so she held it by the blade in her right hand and moved it against her left arm. To operate a successful sawing motion she had to slide it under her raincoat sleeve. It was a very sharp knife; he had chosen well. She cut her arm through her courtelle sweater, but she cut through the cord, too, and her hands were free. She bent to cut the cord round her ankles; then she looked toward the shed. He had come out of it and was running back to her.

Kate acted automatically. Her movements were still restricted, for her thighs were lashed together and though her hands were loose, cords still crossed her chest, holding her upper arms against her body. She could reach the clutch and the accelerator, and he had left the key in the ignition. She started the engine, slammed the gear lever into reverse, and then found she could not move freely enough to see where she was going backward, so she changed into first gear and went forward, toward Gary. His hands were outstretched and he yelled at her. She had no intention of running him down, only of escaping, and tried to pull the car

150

round in a circle, but with her elbows still pinned against her body she had not enough leverage to avoid him altogether, and Gary, as she tried to swerve away from him, leaped in the same direction. She hit him hard with the wing of the car and there was a great thud as he vanished from her sight.

Kate carried on: she completed her circle and drove up the track as fast as the Mini would go, which was not very fast since the slope was steep and she had to stay in low gear. When she reached the top, she stopped and looked back. She could not see him.

She drove on a little way, then stopped again, opened the door, and sat there gasping. After a while she swung her legs out, so that she sat sideways, and cut the rest of the rope away, then rubbed her wrists and legs, ignoring the blood trickling down her left arm. Soon she was able to stand up, and she walked about, stamping her feet to restore the circulation. She leaned against the car then, feeling rather sick and faint, breathing deeply.

Had she killed him?

17

Gary lay winded on the ground. He had struck his head and was briefly stunned; his right arm hurt, and as he struggled to sit up, the pain was more intense than any he had ever known. He could not move it; it hung useless from the shoulder. He sat there whimpering and trembling. That cow: she'd driven straight at him, meant to kill him, when he'd been kind to her. He'd hardly touched her, except to tie her up. He'd shown her every consideration and promised not to hurt her. Why go for him like that? And how in hell had she got free? He'd trusted her, and now this had happened.

She'd be on her way down that lane, gone to fetch the police, for sure.

With the first shock wearing off, Gary tried to think. Once she'd got down the lane, she'd have to find a telephone box. That might not take long, but she'd have to explain where she was, and Gary did not think she knew that any more than he did. He could still get away.

He got to his feet, with difficulty, holding his broken arm with the sound one. Then he lurched toward the nearer hut and leaned against its wall, sweat pouring off him from the effort. Now he became aware of pain in his chest as he breathed and thought at once that it must be his heart. It was pounding and racing; the pain came as his chest rose and fell. His knee hurt, too; the car had caught the whole right side of his body and bounced him off; most of the damage had been caused as he landed.

Cradling his right arm with his left, Gary began to stagger up the rutted track. His light shoes slipped and slithered on the shiny chalk ground. If he could reach the top before the police came, he would strike across the fields and eventually he'd meet a road. Someone might give him a lift, take him to a hospital.

He wouldn't give up. Once on the road, he'd invent a tale about an accident—a hit-and-run. In fact, it was the truth of what had happened.

Gary wasn't used to walking far, and he was in shock. He made slow progress up the slope.

Kate sat for a time in the car with the door open and her feet outside on the ground, her head down to counteract the faintness. Then she realized that blood was flowing down her arm from her self-inflicted wound. Her sweater had, to some extent, protected her arm, but when she took her raincoat off and rolled up the sweater sleeve she found a nasty cut, long and deep, bleeding freely; it looked as if it might need stitching.

She had a small first-aid kit in the car, bought years ago and never used. In it, she found dressings and a bandage. The wound was on her left forearm; she was able to bind it up, though awkwardly, and fixing the bandage was difficult. She could feel

153

that the cut was still bleeding, and when she had put her raincoat on again, she held her arm up so the blood should drain away from it. She still felt rather faint and sick. Then she remembered that there was a tin of barley sugar in the car, in the door pocket. The sweets were old and stuck together; she put three into her mouth; the glucose should help to pull her round.

The wise thing to do was to drive away now, and fetch the police. She walked to the edge of the quarry where Gary had stood earlier, and when she found the sheds were not visible she moved along until she could see them. She could distinguish no figure lying on the ground, and her gaze traveled to the foot of the track. There he was, staggering up it, head down, one hand cupping the elbow of the other arm.

He was by no means dead, but he did not look a very formidable adversary now; besides, she had the knife.

She returned to the car. If he heard the engine, he would realize she had not yet gone for help, but the Mini was on the slight downward incline at the approach to the quarry, so that now it faced a gentle slope. She got in, took the hand brake off, and very slowly the car began to slide away from the edge of the quarry. She let it run until it had gathered some momentum, then switched on and slid it into top gear. The engine was still warm and it fired at once. She drove on until she had rounded the first bend in the lane and was hidden from the quarry top by a hedge, then stopped again.

He was frightened of the countryside. He wouldn't enjoy walking through it alone. It was his turn now to be afraid and suffer.

Gary at last blundered to the top of the quarry. He had stumbled on the slippery, uneven ground, and had fallen, hurting his bad arm again; his chest was more painful now, a twinge catching him

154

with each breath he took. He stood at the end of the track, swaying slightly, looking around and wondering which way to go. Ahead lay the lane along which he had driven with his prisoner and, walking forward, he saw footpaths going off in several directions. All were narrow, leading through bushes to who knew what horrors. There could even be a bull.

He must not take the lane, for the police would come that way. Which should it be, left or right?

While he was wondering, he heard the sudden noise of a car engine; it accelerated loudly. The police already! Instinctively he ducked, but there was no cover and he turned back to the quarry again.

Kate roared up the hill toward him in reverse; she had not been able to turn in the narrow lane. She saw him disappear down the quarry and she parked the Mini so that it was sideways across the mouth of the track; then she got out and looked down. Gary was limping along as fast as he could.

"It's no good running away," Kate called after him. "You can't escape. Come back."

Gary stopped and turned. He saw her standing there above him, a tall figure in a shabby beige raincoat, straight hair framing a face whose expression he could not see from so far away. She looked like a terrible avenging angel in a picture that had frightened him in childhood. One hand was thrust into the pocket of her coat. There was no sign of the police.

He had two choices: to obey her or to go back down the quarry. She might drive down after him—finish what she had tried to do before—run over him properly.

"Come up," Kate called peremptorily.

Gary stood a hundred feet below her. If he went all the way down and she did not, after all, follow and run over him, to escape he would have to climb back again. At the moment he felt

155

that he could not do it if his life depended on it. It didn't, but it might depend on getting medical aid for his chest; the pain when he breathed terrified him.

He began to walk slowly back.

Kate stood there, watching. She felt curiously detached, as if she were a spectator apart from the scene; she felt also a novel sense of power. So that he had room to emerge from the track, she moved the car a little way, turning it to face back along the lane. Then she got out again, and waited beside it.

Gary's ascent took quite a time. When he reached the top, he stopped at the mouth of the track. His hair was wet with sweat and his face was dirty; his clothes were torn and dusty.

Kate waited.

He approached slowly, holding his right arm with his left hand, his feet scuffling through the short grass. Kate had intended to make him walk ahead of her down the lane while she followed slowly in the car. After a mile or so of that, there would be no fight left in him.

She saw that there was none now.

"My—my chest hurts," he croaked.

"You're very unfit," she said disapprovingly, like a stern schoolmistress. "Take off your jacket," she added as he drew near.

He let go of his injured arm and with the other hand began to undo the buttons. Kate saw at once that his upper arm, or possibly the shoulder, was broken. She stood still, not moving an inch to meet him, tall and implacable. Gary stumbled the last little distance toward her.

"Your good arm first, she said, helping him ease his jacket off.

"My chest," he complained again.

"I expect you've broken a few ribs," said Kate without sympathy. She would not tell him that she had not meant to hit him. Let him think what he liked. She was avenging not only herself;

156

there was that poor girl who had lost her life and the only penalty in law that this man would pay would be a few years in prison. He had a future.

"Can I sit down?" Gary asked meekly.

Kate indicated that he might sit in the passenger seat of the car, where she had so lately been a prisoner.

"Face me," she directed, and he obeyed, sitting with his feet on the grass, his back to the steering wheel. Kate stood over him, caught his right forearm, and pulled it across his chest. He yelped. "Hold it there," Kate said. "Go on. Your other arm's working. I'm going to fix a sling."

There was a scarf in her raincoat pocket. She folded it, slipped one end under his forearm, and tied it around his neck. The brown curling hair grew low on it, and was soaked with perspiration.

"Take off your shoes," said Kate next.

He looked up at her. She was only a woman, though a tall one. For an instant he thought of getting up, rushing at her, and by sheer strength pushing her over the quarry edge. Then he saw her hand go to her pocket and he knew she had the knife.

Kate, too, thought for a moment that he might spring at her; she had been foolish to turn her back to the quarry. But he had no spirit left. He bent down and obediently removed his thin and dusty shoes. There was a hole in one sock, the toe showing through rubbed sore by his progress up the quarry track.

Kate put the shoes on the bonnet of the car. Then she picked up his jacket and took out his wallet. She removed two five-pound notes and replaced the wallet in his pocket. Then she held the jacket out to him.

"Put it on," she said. "The good arm only. We'll button it over the other." Some professional concern automatically came into her voice as she said this, but he shrank away from her as if

157

already hurt again. "What a coward you are," she had to add, and knew that this was why he had got himself into the whole predicament.

She buttoned his jacket over the sling and tucked the empty sleeve into the pocket. Then she tied his ankles together, very firmly, with a piece of the cord that had previously bound her.

"Now turn round and get in properly," she said.

He obeyed, and she leaned over to fasten the seat belt. She put his shoes in the back of the car, and she shut the door, locking it. His left arm was free, but he was genuinely in pain and suffering from shock. He would not escape. If he tried, he would get nowhere in that condition, without shoes. She got in beside him, his money in her pocket along with the knife.

18

Detective Inspector Bailey was in his office drinking a cup of tea. He had just held a meeting with the press and revealed that the police wanted to interview Gary Browne, aged twenty-four. He had described the wanted man; photofit pictures were released. This was a case where the press could be very useful, and when questions were fired at Bailey he had not been evasive. However, until the messenger from Ferringham arrived with samples of prints found in the house from which Kate Wilson had disappeared, no mention of a possible link between the incidents could be made. Marvellous, isn't it, he thought, that a car's ownership could be proved by computer in seconds, rockets could go to the moon, but fingerprints had to be delivered. Meanwhile, the coincidences were being explored; a detective had gone to The Black Swan, and a cast of the footprint found in Kent was on its way. The pieces of the jigsaw were coming together, but a nationwide hunt might be needed to find Browne, and if he had abducted Kate Wilson, she might die before he was caught.

He was crunching his digestive biscuit when Frith bounded into the room.

"Sir! Sir! You won't believe this," he cried. "Some woman's just been on the blower to say she's got the bloke who killed Sandra King in her car. Says she's on her way here. Didn't give her name—or his."

Bailey looked sourly at the sergeant.

"Well, go on," he said. "Pull the other one."

"I know, sir," said Frith. "But she says she'll be here within an hour. She wants no help."

"Where is she, Frith?"

"Wouldn't say. She was calling from a box," said Frith. "Said we weren't to worry."

"We won't," Bailey answered.

Kate put the telephone down knowing she had done nothing to let anyone in Ferringham know that she was safe. She could not imagine, though, that her mother would be feeling anxious about anything except her own comfort, and by now Mrs. Burke or the police would have made some arrangements about that. The Health Centre would be managing, too; no one was indispensable. If Richard was worried—and she hoped he was—he would survive for a few more hours. She would be home that night.

She had decided to take her prisoner back to Wattleton, where he had committed his original crime. Let him be arrested there, for that offense, and let his abduction of herself take a secondary place, if it had to be proceeded with at all. She would want him charged on her account only if it would increase his sentence for what he had done to Sandra King.

They drove northward, by-passing Reading and cutting across

160

Buckinghamshire, not hurrying, and keeping away from main roads. They circled towns. Kate did not want to attract attention. They must look like any couple in a Mini harmlessly pursuing their own concerns. The police, if they were searching for her, would not, she thought, be looking for a woman driver.

They met no patrols.

They stopped for petrol at a service station where Kate brushed at herself to tidy herself before she got out and stood beside the attendant, masking the car's number plate, while he filled the tank. She paid with some of Gary's money, then drove off. The attendant took no notice of the silent male figure in the passenger's seat. If he had, he would merely have seen a man with a jacket buttoned over an arm in a sling. The knotted feet could not be seen.

Kate was very thirsty but she decided not to buy any food or drink. Fluid created problems. She did not speak at all. When Gary asked where they were going, she did not answer.

He moaned now and then. Kate knew he was in pain, but she was sure his injuries were not serious. Aspirins might have relieved him, but she had none.

They had been on the road for a long time before Gary understood: he saw a Risely signpost.

Kate went through the village, past the service station, and stopped at a call box beyond it. From there she telephoned Wattleton Central Police Station, using some change from the petrol money. She found the number in the telephone directory; dialing 999 would not, she felt, bring her into contact with whoever was working on the case of Sandra King.

She was passed, in the suburbs of Wattleton, by a white police Ford Escort in which was the constable who had been sent to inquire about lone ladies spending the weekend at The Black

Swan. She followed him. The chances were that he was bound, also, for police headquarters.

"It's her! It's Kate Wilson! That's who it was rang up. She's downstairs and she's got him with her—Gary Browne!"

Frith had burst once again into Detective Inspector Bailey's office.

"What—?"

"It's right, sir. Drove in behind P. C. Stanley, who's been over to Risely. Followed him into the yard and blew her Mini horn—toot, toot," mimicked Frith, beside himself. "We've got Browne in an interview room," he added, more soberly. "And the doctor's on his way—Browne's hurt. Young Berry's with him, and Stanley's looking after Miss Wilson. It is her all right, sir. It's her Mini, the number we had from the Ferringham law, though she's got no personal identification on her. It's Browne, too—spitting image of the photofits."

"Has he confessed?" asked Bailey, when he could speak.

"Not yet, sir. We thought it best he should wait for you," said Frith. "He will, I'd say. Had a rough time of it, by the look of him."

Kate's statement took some time to make. She offered to write it herself, but Frith said no, an officer would do it for her. The proceedings seemed to go on forever, though the police were kind enough. Kate described everything that had happened from Friday evening onward; the only thing she left out was any mention of Richard, saying simply that she spent occasional weekends at The Black Swan.

"Perhaps it's an offense to use a false name," she said. This was the hardest part. "I began staying away when I was younger. My mother—we live together—would not have approved of the expense, so I pretended to be visiting a friend. This friend always knew where I was, in case my mother was ill—she's elderly and not strong. I used the false name because I'm—er—I'm not a very sophisticated person, Sergeant, and it gave me confidence to pretend to be a widow."

"I see, Miss Wilson." Frith showed no surprise and asked her to continue with her story.

It was Detective Chief Superintendent Hawksworth, entering while the interview was still in progress, who said, "We've told the Ferringham police you're safe, Miss Wilson. Would you like to telephone Dr. Stearne yourself?"

Kate, until now so calm, stared at both the men.

"Dr. Stearne?" she said faintly.

"He got in touch with Chief Inspector Meredith at Ferringham as soon as he realized your disappearance might be connected with the death of Sandra King," said Hawksworth. "Up here, we didn't know about you, you see. And without Dr. Stearne's information the Ferringham police wouldn't have connected the two incidents. We'd have got there, in the end, but not yet." The trail of Gary Browne would eventually have led them to his new car, left in a Ferringham street and now in police custody, containing among other items a pair of rubber gloves which Ferringham's C.I.D. said might yield interesting information.

"Oh," said Kate. "Richard—he did that?"

"Yes, Miss Wilson," said Hawksworth. He looked at the bedraggled woman in her shabby raincoat. Her motives for bringing Gary Browne back to Wattleton were quite clear to him, but that did not diminish her achievement.

Kate, in fact, hadn't done it all for Richard; she had proved something to herself, too.

"Would you let him know, please," she said. "I'll be in to work as usual tomorrow, you could say." Her voice was steady again. It could all still be kept quiet if the police were the only ones who knew. This older man seemed sympathetic.

"You've been very brave, Miss Wilson, if somewhat unwise," said Hawksworth. "You should have gone for help when you'd got away from Browne in the quarry."

"I know—I've explained all that." Kate cast a despairing glance at Frith. "I wanted you to deal with him—in Wattleton. I want to be left out of it, if possible. I didn't mean to hit him with the car," she added. "That was an accident. He's broken an arm and cracked some ribs, but I don't think he's seriously hurt."

"No, he isn't. The doctor's seen him, and he'll be going to hospital to be X-rayed, but we'll have him back after that, safely under lock and key."

"Oh, is there a doctor here?" asked Kate. "Perhaps he'd just look at my arm. I think I need some stitches. I did it myself, getting free. He didn't hurt me. What did you say his name was?"

No one had told her. She had called him nothing during the hours they had spent together, and he had addressed her by a false name, yet they had shown each other more of their true natures than they had, perhaps, to any other living soul.

"For goodness' sake, Frith!" Now Hawksworth looked angry. "Didn't you know Miss Wilson was injured? Go and see if the doctor's gone, and if he has, take her to the hospital at once."

Kate said, diffidently, "Please could I have some tea?"

A woman police constable drove Kate back to Ferringham.

"But why can't I just go back quietly on my own?" she asked.

She was told that her car must be examined. It would be returned as soon as the lab had finished with it.

"But he's admitted everything, hasn't he?"

Gary had confessed to killing Sandra King, though by accident, and to abducting Kate with malicious intent.

164

"We must have proof for the court," she was told, and then the news about her mother's stroke was broken to her.

"It wasn't a major one," said the young woman who was taking her home. "But of course it's serious, especially at her age. It's not known yet how much permanent damage has been done. They'll tell you more at the hospital."

Now, riding along, her arm stitched and bound up firmly, Kate said, "I'll have to go and see my mother. If you can spare the time, could we possibly call in at the hospital?"

"Of course," said the policewoman. "But don't you want a bath and a change of clothes first? I'll wait and run you to the hospital after that."

"Suppose she dies, and I haven't been to see her?" said Kate. "She won't be surprised if I'm a bit untidy. I often am." She had washed at the police station, and been lent a comb.

At Ferringham Hospital, the policewoman went with Kate to where, in her amenity bed, Mrs. Wilson lay in isolation. She seemed to be asleep, but woke when a nurse gently touched her arm.

"Here's your daughter, Mrs. Wilson. Back safe and sound."

One baleful eye glared at Kate; the other drooped. The face was slightly twisted, but the words that emerged slowly from the quavering mouth could be understood.

"Fancy going off like that and leaving me alone," said Mrs. Wilson. "How could you be so thoughtless?"

"She doesn't understand," said the nurse, patting Mrs. Wilson's hand in mild reproof and putting it under the bedclothes. "She will in a day or two, when she feels stronger."

But Kate knew that however good her mother's eventual recovery, she would always be blamed for what had happened.

Jeremy King was told by Detective Chief Superintendent Hawksworth himself that Sandra's assailant had been caught.

When the doorbell rang, Jeremy was sitting in the chair where, had he but known it, Sandra had sat refusing to join Gary on the sofa. He was staring at the spot where she had died.

"May I come in a minute, Mr. King?" said Hawksworth when Jeremy opened the door; and moving on into the living room, he sat down on the sofa. "Mind if I sit down?" he added. The young man must get used to seeing someone in that place. "It's been a long day. For you, too."

"Er—yes." Jeremy made an effort to concentrate. "Would you like a drink, Mr. Hawksworth? I've got some beer."

He'd gone to fetch some earlier, finding none in the flat. It had occupied a little time.

"Thank you," said Hawksworth, and sat waiting while Jeremy rummaged about in the kitchen, finally emerging with bottles and glasses.

When each had taken a ritual sip, Hawksworth spoke.

"Well, we've got him, Mr. King," he said. "He'll be charged in the morning."

"Gary Browne? It was him? The salesman?"

"No doubt about it," said Hawksworth.

Browne would be charged with murder, but a clever lawyer might put the cat among the pigeons, alleging provocation, and so obtain a verdict of manslaughter and a relatively short sentence, but there was no need for the widower to know that now.

"That won't bring Sandra back, will it?" said Jeremy bleakly. "Nor her reputation. Some people are already saying she may have asked for it."

The previous morning at the inquest, which had been adjourned, Jeremy had overheard such comment.

"You don't believe that, do you, Mr. King?" asked Hawksworth.

"No. Why did she fight him, if that were true?" said Jeremy, but his words were firmer than the tone in which they were uttered.

166

"Folk are quick to believe the worst," said Hawksworth.

Jeremy recalled his own suspicions of Bill Ogden; he had doubted Sandra, too; he was no better than anyone else.

"I still can't really believe that I'll never see her again," he said. "She—what she went through—she must have been so frightened."

There was no answer to this.

"What sort of man is he, this Gary Browne?" Jeremy asked. "Is he—is he—clean?"

"Oh, yes." Hawksworth instantly understood the implication of the question. Gary Browne had been far from clean when delivered to Wattleton Central Police Station, but under the lacerations, the dust, and the grime, there had been the wreck of a spruce young man. His good appearance would not help stem malicious talk about his victim when he came to court.

"It's something, I suppose," said Jeremy. "You see, she was very fastidious."

Hawksworth let a moment or two pass in silence before he spoke again.

"He's got a broken arm and some very painful broken ribs," he said then. "He was in a road accident."

"Good. Pity he didn't break his bloody neck," said Jeremy. "Was anyone else hurt?"

"No," said Hawksworth. "Well—a slight cut and some shock. Nothing to matter at all." Time enough for Jeremy to learn the details later.

Hawksworth had had a long talk with Chief Inspector Meredith on the telphone. Kate's part in the affair would be played down as far as possible, but Browne would have to be charged with his offense against her and the press would love it.

"Is he mad—Gary Browne?" asked Jeremy.

"No," said Hawksworth. "He panicked. She started to scream and he meant to silence her, not kill her. He simply saw no reason he shouldn't have something he wanted. That's the creed of too many people these days, Mr. King. Grab, and hang to anyone else." He paused. "The papers will make a meal of it all and it will be very unpleasant, but it'll soon blow over. Some other piece of news will be on the front pages."

"They've been trying to talk to me," said Jeremy." The reporters. I've been pretty rude."

"They can take it," said Hawksworth. "We'll be putting out a statement later. Inspector Bailey's working on it now. I hope you won't have too much trouble, though some are bound to look for the personal angle."

"The funeral's on Friday," said Jeremy. "That's personal. I'll tell them that."

Kate slept well. She had never before been alone in the house. In the morning, she rang the hospital. Her mother had spent a comfortable night and was a little stronger. Kate said she would come in during evening visiting hours.

She had breakfast, with fresh coffee instead of her normal instant, a boiled egg, and an extra slice of toast. There v as no hurry now. The paper, on an inside page, reported that a man had been arrested in connection with the death of Sandra King and would appear in court that morning. Her name did not appear.

With a head scarf over her hair, and in her beige raincoat, but wearing beneath it a green woolen dress of Mrs. Havant's—for those clothes would now no longer be hidden—she went to work on her bicycle, still kept in the garage and needing only a little air in the front tire.

She parked it in the yard at the Health Centre where staff and patients alike left their cars, chaining it to a rail. She was, as usual, the first to arrive, apart from the cleaner.

"Oh, Miss Wilson—you're back. That's good. How's your poor mother?" asked the cleaner.

"Better, thank you," Kate replied.

"Marvelous, isn't she?" said the cleaner, who had never met Mrs. Wilson. "I heard she'd been took bad—I wondered why you weren't here yesterday."

Well, here was someone who did not know what had really happened.

Kate put on her white coat and went into the office, where everything was in order, as she expected. Marjorie Dodds was perfectly capable of carrying on.

She began her routine work, opening the letters, and then she heard their cars arrive: Dr. Wetherbee's Rover, which he drove straight to his special spot under the window: Richard's Peugeot, which he always reversed against the wall; then Paul, in his MGB, making the exhaust snort as he spun in a circle before drawing up next to the entrance. Silly man, she thought, slitting open a letter from the Ministry of Health; he's middle-aged, with a son as tall as himself and two smaller lads; he should have a comfortable family car instead of pretending to be young.

Kate was still opening letters when the three doctors came into the office together, looking rather like a deputation. Dr. Wetherbee spoke first.

"Kate—how are you?" he asked, his tone brisk but his face showing the kindly concern Kate had known from him all her life.

"Quite all right," said Kate.

"Should you be here?"

"Yes, really. I'm better working," said Kate.

"Very well, my dear. I'll see you later," said Dr. Wetherbee, and he left the room.

The other two men remained.

"Well, Kate, you gave us quite a fright, I must say," said Paul.

169

"I'm glad you escaped a fate worse than death." He did not seem to understand that she had, in fact, escaped death itself. He leaned over and put a hand on her shoulder. Kate suddenly noticed how ugly it was, thick and red, with ginger hair sprouting along the back of it, his fingers like raw sausages. Why had she never noticed that before? "Well, I won't play gooseberry," Paul went on. "I'm sure you two have plenty to talk about." He put one of those fat hands up in the air. "Bless you, my children," he said, with a leer, and as he went out, he closed the door ostentatiously behind him.

Kate said nothing, but she laid down her paper knife and clasped her hands together. There was a red mark on one wrist, a spot rubbed raw as she had worked to free her bound hands. Richard knew at once what it was. He longed to take her in his arms and kiss the little wound. But they were in the office, and anyone might enter.

"Oh, Kate!" he said, instead, and she had never heard his voice sound like that before.

"Paul knows," said Kate. "Who else?"

"Well—everyone will soon, I suppose," said Richard. "The police do—I don't know who else. But that doesn't matter now. You're safe. That's what counts."

"It does matter, Richard. Cynthia—your whole life—could be destroyed. I think it will be all right. He—Browne—confessed. I've explained that I sometimes stayed at The Black Swan under an assumed name because of my mother. That's all that need be known to explain why I was involved. So it needn't come out if Paul keeps quiet. How did he find out?"

"I told him," Richard said.

Kate stared at him.

"What a stupid thing to do," she said. "Whatever made you be so foolish?" She pressed her lips together in case they trembled and betrayed her.

170

Richard stared at her. Where was his gentle, silly Kate?

"Oh, a variety of reasons," he said. On the telephone the evening before, he had learned from Detective Chief Superintendent Hawksworth most of Kate's story; at the moment when he was quareling with Paul, she was already safe at Wattleton. "It will have to come out," he added.

"No," said Kate. "That man—Browne—broke into a shop in Kent looking for me, and there's some woman in Hammersmith who stayed at The Black Swan, too. She had a mystery caller selling encyclopedias. She saw him through a spyhole and can identify him. He was seen by a couple in her block of flats, too. Browne admitted going there. There's lots of proof to send him down. You needn't be involved."

She had even picked up the police jargon during her stay with Hawksworth and his men.

"You must be exhausted," Richard said. "You shouldn't have come in today." Her icy manner must be the result of shock. "What about your arm?" Hawksworth had told him about that.

"It's all right. Much better not disturb the dressing," said Kate, in case he thought of doing so. She was not sure what would happen if he touched her. "Thank you for telling the police about The Black Swan, Richard."

"Well, of course I told them, as soon as I realized there might be a connection," Richard said. "What did you expect me to do? Let you be killed? I was afraid it was too late anyway."

Richard's efforts had not helped her. She had won her own safety, and had played high stakes to protect him; now he was throwing away that part of what she had done.

"What did you tell Cynthia yesterday?"

"Nothing. It wasn't necessary." She'd assumed an emergency call had interrupted his lunch when she found it abandoned.

"Paul's the only risk, then," said Kate. "You should be able to keep him quiet without much trouble. He had an affair with that gallstone patient of his two years ago—Mrs. Bowen, her name is. And there have been others. I can tell you who they were. He's seeing rather a lot of Sybil Meadows at the moment. So there's no need to worry about him."

"Kate!"

"You'd hate to be forced to marry me, if Cynthia found out. And if she did, you might feel that you should," said Kate. She picked up the paper knife again. "We're not cut out for one another full time. I'm not really Mrs. Havant, remember. I'm just Kate."

"No—Kate—my dear—" Richard felt a surge of real grief. She meant what she was saying. It was over, just like that. Then, oddly, beneath the sorrow flickered faint relief. One day, it would have had to end, perhaps peter out sadly, like a long fatal illness. Sudden death was often kinder.

"If Cynthia hears some rumor, she won't believe it," Kate said. "She won't want to. She'll think it's just gossip. You can say you hadn't bothered to mention seeing me at The Black Swan as it wasn't important."

Her mother must be prevented from hearing malicious speculation, too: her illness should make that easy.

"It was important, Kate," said Richard. "Very."

Kate picked up the next envelope in the pile of mail.

"Yes," she said. "It was. For a time."

172